Alone for Christmas

FROM BESTSELLING AUTHOR

ASHLEY JOHN

Cover designed by Ashley Mcloughlin
Edited by Keri Lierman

1st Edition: November 21st 2016.

For questions and comments about this book, please contact the author at hi@ashleyjohn.co.uk.

ISBN: 1540552489
ISBN-13: 978-1540552488

ALSO BY ASHLEY JOHN

Standalone Novels

Alone For Christmas

Ricky

Timing

Cabin Nights

Shelter

BOSS

Surf Bay

Lost & Found

Full Circle

Saving Michael

Love's Medicine

Sink or Swim

George & Harvey

The Secret

The Truth

The Fight

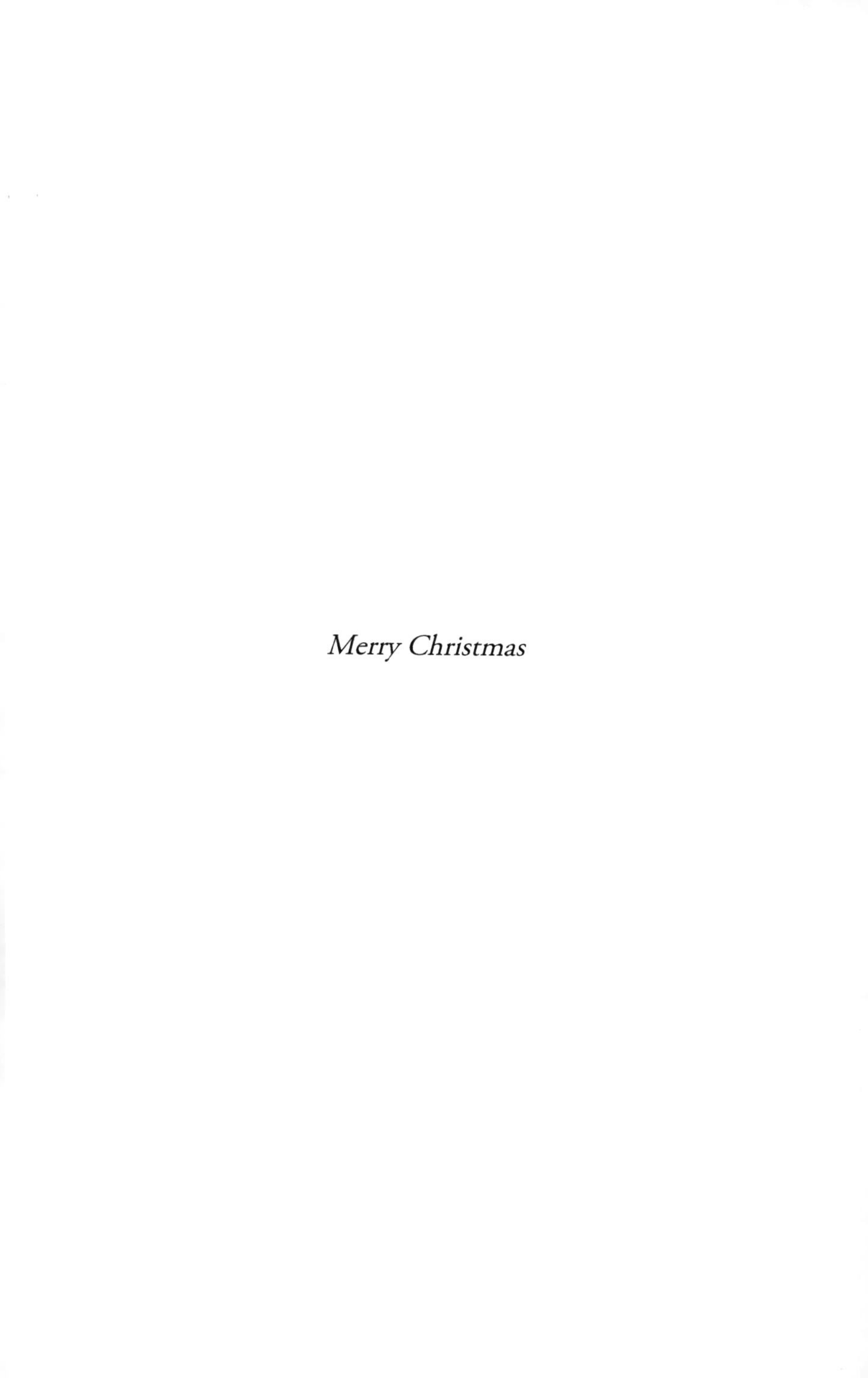

Merry Christmas

CHAPTER *One*

Noah scratched at the tight reindeer ears in his ginger hair as he cast an eye over to his boss's office. It had been twenty minutes since Chip Harington's soon to be ex-wife had stormed into the office demanding to see her husband, and things were suspiciously quiet.

"I wonder if she's killed him," whispered Amy in the next cubicle. "They're usually arguing by now."

"Don't say that," said Noah. "I wouldn't put it past her."

"I was joking."

"I wasn't." Noah pursed his lips and arched a brow down at Amy, his best friend and only fellow redhead in the entire office. "She's probably holding him upside down and shaking every last coin out of him."

"Like the second wife, you mean?" said Amy with a smirk as she resumed typing her email. "Don't worry. I think your lover boy will live to see another day."

"He's not my lover boy," said Noah, the blood rushing to his pale cheeks.

"But you wish he was."

Noah regretted ever telling Amy about the crush he had on their boss. She brought it up every chance she got, making him realise how stupid he was for spending most nights imagining them in bed together. With a boss as attractive as Chip Harington, it was impossible to imagine anything else.

The door to Chip's office suddenly opened and Noah swiftly sat down and started typing. Sasha Harington reappeared with black mascara streaks running down her rouged cheeks. Noah had never liked her, but even he didn't like the thought of somebody being that upset two days before Christmas. With her long blonde hair cascading down her face, she headed straight for the door.

Noah looked down at the gibberish he had been typing before looking up again, just in time to catch Chip's hazel eyes, before he slammed his office door and closed the blinds.

The sound of heavy typing suddenly stopped in the office and it was replaced by hushed whispering. Amy popped up over the wall of his cubicle, her red hair draping over the pictures of the two of them on various nights out in London.

"Tonight's Christmas party is going to be interesting," she whispered with a devilish grin. "That's if he even shows up."

Noah grumbled his agreement in his throat as he deleted the nonsense typing one letter at a time. He glanced over to Chip's office again, wondering how somebody so handsome could be divorcing for a third time before the age of forty.

By the time the clock struck five, the office was almost emptied. Amy stood up and stretched out before wrapping a thick, yellow scarf around her neck and pulling on her trench coat.

"Fancy a quick drink at the pub?" she asked as she pulled her reindeer ears out of her red curls. "I can probably spare half an hour before I need to start getting ready."

"I'm going to finish up some things here first," he said without looking away from the screen as he continued to type. "I've got to finalise Johnny Wood's contract before the new year and I'd rather finish it before Christmas."

"Your funeral," she sighed as she pulled her

cigarettes from her handbag. "I'll see you tonight."

"Yeah," he mumbled. "See you later."

Amy flicked off her cubicle light, placed a cigarette between her lips and headed for the door. When it closed, Noah stopped typing and looked around the office. The only light was coming from his cubicle and Chip's office.

He looked back at the publishing contract. The words blurred together as he let out a long yawn. The thought of having to spend the night drinking with his co-workers in a bar didn't interest him tonight, but he knew he couldn't miss it.

Half an hour later, he finished proofreading the contract for the third time, and when he was satisfied, he sent it to the printer. Standing up, he stretched out and yawned again as he looked at Chip's closed office blinds. He hadn't resurfaced since Sasha had run out of his office crying and Noah hadn't been able to think of much else all day.

When the printer spat out its final piece of paper, Noah gathered the contract and enclosed it neatly in a cardboard sleeve. He quickly scribbled '*Johnny Wood's Revised Publishing Contract*' on the front and turned off his computer.

After he grabbed his leather jacket and laptop bag from under his desk, he flicked off his cubicle light. He thought about keeping hold of the contract over the Christmas break and reading through it again before handing it over to Chip. He pulled on his jacket and almost put the folder in his bag, but he decided against it.

Rifling through the stack of papers to make sure he hadn't missed anything, he walked over to Chip's office door, but he paused before knocking. He knew Chip wouldn't care about the contract, considering the eventful couple of weeks he had had. Noah didn't know how news of his divorce had leaked to the office, but it was all people had been able to talk about in the run up to Christmas.

Before Noah could chicken out, he knocked heavily on the frosted glass in the door and took a step back into darkness. He waited for a response, or any sound of life inside of the office, but there wasn't one.

"Mr. Harington," Noah called through the wood as he knocked again. "It's just Noah. I have the Johnny Wood contract you wanted me to look over."

Thirty seconds of silence followed, so Noah got the message. Deciding his boss didn't want to see anyone, he bent down and pushed the folder through the gap underneath the door. As he straightened back up, the door quickly opened and bright, fluorescent light flooded the darkness.

Chip Harington stood in the door, a frown on his brow, casting a heavy shadow over his deep, hazel eyes. He squinted into the dark at Noah, who took a step forward. Chip's eyes glanced up to the reindeer ears in

Noah's ginger hair. Embarrassed, Noah quickly pulled them off.

"What are you doing here, Noah?" Chip asked with vulnerability in his voice that Noah had never heard before. "I thought everybody had gone home."

"I just wanted to get this finished before the Christmas break," he said, quickly scrambling down to pick up the contract he had pushed under the door.

Chip stepped to the side and walked over to his desk, leaving the office door open. Noah took it as an invitation, so he followed Chip into the bright office and placed the paperwork on the desk, next to a half-empty bottle of Jameson Whiskey. Noah wondered how full the bottle had been at the beginning of the day.

With a heavy exhale, Chip collapsed into his leather desk chair and pinched between his brows. It was rare Noah ever saw him in anything other than a sharp, designer suit, but today was one of those days. His tie had been pulled loose and it hung by his half-open shirt, which showed off the light speckling of hair on his broad, muscled chest.

"You're a hard worker, Noah," said Chip softly, a small smile forcing its way through his pained expression. "Not many people would stay behind on the night of the Christmas party to get something finished."

"It's my job, sir," he said.

"Not everybody thinks like that." Chip dropped the hand from his face and looked directly into Noah's eyes. "I appreciate it."

Noah was beginning to think Chip had forgotten all about the contract until he picked it up. He flicked through it for a moment, but Noah wasn't sure if he was even reading. Either way, he seemed satisfied by what he was looking at, and he opened his top drawer and dropped the document inside.

"Good work," he said as he sat up, unscrewing the cap on the bottle of Jameson. "Get yourself home, Noah."

"Yes, sir," said Noah quietly as he watched Chip pour himself a Jameson. "See you at the Christmas party?"

Chip stopped pouring and looked up at Noah with an arched brow. For a moment, Noah thought he had landed himself in trouble, but Chip just smirked and gently shook his head.

"I doubt I would be much fun," he said, taking a sip of his whiskey. "You'll all have more fun without me."

"I doubt that, sir," said Noah, taking a step back to the door. "You've earned this party just as much as everybody else in this office."

Chip narrowed his eyes over the top of his whiskey glass and stared at Noah, amusement in his gaze. He closed his eyes, tossed back the whiskey and sat up in his chair.

Deciding he had overstayed his welcome, Noah turned around and headed for the door. Before he reached it, he noticed the sleeping bag on the couch under the window, and an open bag of men's toiletries. Glancing over his shoulder at his boss, he almost made a comment but thought better of it, deciding to just say, "Goodnight, sir."

CHAPTER *Two*

"Sleeping in his office?" asked Amy as she exhaled cigarette smoke through her nose like a dragon. "Are you sure?"

"Why else would there be a sleeping bag?"

Noah wafted the smoke out of his face and climbed over the mess in his flat to open a window. He tripped on the wire of the fairy lights on his pathetically small Christmas tree, which dropped to the floor.

"It's probably for the best," said Amy as he picked

up the tiny Christmas tree and set it back on the side table. "It's hardly the *John Lewis* vision of Christmas in here."

"This is my first Christmas alone," he said as he straightened the £1 angel on top of the tiny tree. "I'm not in the mood to celebrate."

"I still feel bad about that," said Amy, dropping the lit stub of her cigarette into her almost finished glass of wine. "If my Grandma wasn't so strict about 'family only', I would have invited you to my place."

"It's okay," he said with a wave of his hand, trying not to think too hard about it. "I'm just going to let it pass me by. The only way I'll even know it's Christmas is the crap TV and the silence of the city."

Noah tossed back the last of his white wine. He went to pour himself another glass, but they had polished off an entire bottle in the hour since Amy had turned up in her silver gown.

Amy brushed invisible lint from Noah's shoulder and straightened up his tie with a soft smile on her cherry-red lips.

"You look beautiful," he said as she adjusted his waxed hair for him.

"I should," she chuckled. "Do you know how long it took me to straighten this bush out? Two whole hours! If it weren't for Steve Banks, I wouldn't have bothered."

"Are you still trying to make out with Steve

Banks? You've been trying for the last two Christmases."

"And I feel like this is my year." She stepped back and assessed him with a satisfied nod. "You'll do. You might even get your own kiss under the mistletoe."

Amy pulled a mirror out of her small, silver clutch and reapplied her lipstick for the third time since arriving. He laughed off her suggestion. Noah had always found it difficult to find guys he was sexually attracted to, and the one guy who occupied his fantasies and dreams was straight, divorcing his third wife, and unlikely to show up to his own Christmas party.

"You know Clark in Finance has a thing for you," offered Amy, who had always been able to read what was on his mind. "Beth told me so."

"Clark?" Noah wrinkled his nose. "Which one is he?"

"Glasses and curly hair," she said. "He's cute. Bit nerdy, but cute."

"Beth is probably talking out of her backside, as usual. Remember when she told us she was dating a footballer and we all believed her?"

"Well, he was a footballer," said Amy, "if you count Sunday league down at The Crown pub."

Noah laughed as he picked up his phone and pushed it into his inside pocket. He thought about his last visit to the Finance Department and his brief interaction with Clark. He was pretty new at the office and they had talked about the weather for about forty-five seconds.

"That'll be the taxi!" exclaimed Amy when his intercom speaker buzzed. "How do I look?"

"Snog-worthy," he said, giving her two thumbs up.

"Not shag-worthy then?" she said with a sarcastic wink as she linked her arm with Noah's. "Let's go get pissed and dance the night away."

It suddenly sounded like the only thing he wanted to do, even if he couldn't stop his mind from wandering to Chip Harington spending the evening alone, drinking whiskey in his office before collapsing into his sleeping bag.

The taxi pulled up outside of *Resurrection*, a posh bar in West London that Chip Harington had booked exclusively for Harington Publishing House's Christmas party.

"Bloody hell, this beats last year's art gallery," mumbled Amy as she crawled out of the taxi, an unlit cigarette already pressed between her lips. "Shame ol' Chippy won't be here to enjoy it."

Noah paid the taxi driver and joined Amy on the side of the road outside of the bar as she lit her cigarette. Despite arriving twenty minutes early, music and chattering poured from the busy bar.

"King Harington hasn't shown his face yet," said Beth as she joined them outside the bar, pulling a fur shawl around her shoulders. "I doubt he will after that performance earlier. Poor Sasha, it's her I feel sorry for."

She pulled out an electronic cigarette from her handbag and puffed away as she shivered next to Noah. Amy looked to him and rolled her eyes.

"I heard he cheated on her," added Beth when neither of them picked up her bait.

"Where did you hear that?" Amy scoffed. "Sounds like bullshit to me, Beth."

"I heard what I heard," she said, holding up her hands. "Don't shoot the messenger."

"I don't think he'd cheat," mumbled Noah, almost to himself. "He seems too nice for that."

"They always do," sighed Beth as she dropped her electronic cigarette back into her bag and snapped it shut. "See you two inside."

Amy waited for Beth to go back inside before saying, "Not if I can help it."

When Amy finished her cigarette, they left the cold of the West London street and entered the warm bar. There was already a buzz in the air, Christmas music providing the backdrop for endless chatter and drinking. Noah didn't doubt for a second what the topic of their conversation was.

"Is it a free bar?" Amy called over the music to the

bartender.

"Until midnight," he replied as he wiped the counter. "What can I get you?"

"Tequila shots?" Amy nudged Noah in the ribs. "What better way to get started, eh? Especially if his lordship is paying."

Noah cast an eye around the busy room, waiting for Chip's face to jump out at him. He shook his head to the tequila and opted for a dry white wine instead.

He drained his first free glass of wine and it joined the two generous glasses he had had at his flat. His mind started to ease. Amy had headed straight for Steve the minute she had seen him, leaving him to mingle with his co-workers.

"I told you they'd be divorced before the new year!" said Rodger Barker, an elderly editor who had worked at the publishing house for as long as anyone old enough could remember. "He's just like his father! Goes through women like underwear. The second they start to show a bit of wear, he tosses them out and gets something a little fresher."

"We should do a wager for his next marriage," said Jackie, another of the editors. "Place bets on how many months until the divorce."

Noah sipped his second glass of wine, listening but not wanting to get involved. He didn't know if it was his feelings for his boss that disabled his ability to talk shit about him, or if he just didn't think he deserved it.

Chip Harington was a good man to work for, and they all knew it, so he didn't understand why they all turned on him the second his personal life became the focus. In the two years Noah had been there, this was Chip's second divorce. Amy said it was because they had nothing else going on in their lives, but Noah thought it was more than that. People loved cheap gossip and seeing successful people fail, but he wasn't going to join in the lynch mob.

"I think he falls too fast and hard," said Rodger. "When I met my Judith, we courted for months before we even thought of getting serious. That's how we did it back in the day. Kids these days are too fast to settle down."

"He's not a kid," said Noah, surprised by the sternness in his voice. "He's thirty-two."

"And thrice divorced!" exclaimed Jackie.

They all stood in silence for a moment before Rodger and Jackie wandered away from Noah, leaving him to take a generous gulp of his wine. He glanced over to Amy, who had somehow managed to get Steve on his own on a sofa in a dark corner. He admired her ability to go after things she wanted; it was certainly more than he could do. Laughing to himself, he sipped more of his wine, imagining how his boss would react if he found out about his ridiculous crush. Chip had always been nice to Noah, but he doubted even Chip's kind nature would stretch that far.

Noah tossed back the rest of his drink and dumped his glass. He thought about going over to Amy, but he didn't want to be the reason she had to wait another year to kiss Steve Banks under the mistletoe. He checked his watch, and it was only passing nine in the evening, which meant there were three hours left of a free bar to take advantage of. Deciding Christmas parties were for getting drunk and doing stupid things, he headed back to the bar and hoisted himself up on a stool.

As he drank his third glass of free wine, the party busied around him, and the noise levels rose above the music as the drinks flowed. More than once, he heard people talking about Chip Harington, but he decided to tune it out.

The empty stool next to him was suddenly occupied and he was surprised to see Clark from Finance.

"Good party, right?" asked Clark as he waited to catch the bartender's attention. "Is it like this every year?"

"Chip always puts a lot of effort into the Christmas party," said Noah, noticing the slight slur in his voice. "He takes care of his staff."

"Shame he's not here," said Clark, who seemed to lean in closer to Noah. "Can I buy you a drink?"

"It's a free bar."

"Can I get you a free drink, then?" he chuckled

softly.

Noah drained the last of his third free wine, totalling five glasses altogether. He looked over to Amy, who to his shock, was successfully making out with Steve Banks, and all without the aid of well-placed mistletoe. Knowing that he had lost his best friend for the evening, he accepted Clark's offer of a drink.

As Clark ordered two glasses of wine, Noah stared at the accountant's face. Clark was cute, in a geeky sort of way, but he wasn't Chip Harington. Noah wondered if he could look past that for the sake of a fumble at the Christmas party. He wondered if Beth's gossip about Clark having a crush on him were true. He could almost hear Amy telling him to go for it.

Clark handed Noah a glass of wine, which quickly found its way to his lips.

"So, you're in Legal?" Clark asked as he sipped what seemed to be his first drink of the evening.

"Contracts, small print," he said with a nod, "that sort of thing. It's super boring, but it pays the bills."

"I'm an accountant. Boring is my middle name."

They both shared a laugh, and for a moment, the thought of taking Clark back to his flat didn't seem so farfetched. He knew Clark might not want to, but even Noah could pick up on the subtle leaning and lingering eye contact. He didn't know if it was the wine, or the knowledge that the one man he found attractive didn't share the feeling, but he didn't mind the attention as much as he usually would have.

When he was about to finish the last of his wine and he had finally plucked up the courage to ask Clark back to his flat, an eerie silence shuddered through the party. Clark looked up from his drink, and the easy smile on his lips suddenly vanished as he adjusted his glasses in the direction of the door.

"Fuck me," Clark whispered. "He actually came."

Knowing exactly who Clark was talking about, Noah spun around on his chair so fast, he tumbled backwards, with nothing to grab hold of.

CHAPTER *Three*

Wine mixed with a sharp pain in the back of Noah's head when he opened his eyes. He looked up into the crowd of faces as they blurred and divided. Blinking hard, he tried to steady his thoughts as two sets of arms grabbed him on both sides, pulling him up to his feet.

Suddenly feeling incredibly sober, Noah attempted to shake away the embarrassment that was rushing through his body as he realised that all eyes were on him. Amy pushed her way through the crowd and grabbed his shoulders.

"Are you okay?" she cried over the music.

"I'm fine." Noah shrugged off all of the hands holding onto him and touched the back of his head, which seemed unaffected after colliding with the slate tiles. "I'm an idiot."

"A clumsy idiot," said Amy as she lifted his face up to the light. "How many fingers am I holding up?"

"Leave off, Amy," he said, batting her fingers away. "I'm fine everyone, honestly."

He saw a mixture of amusement and concern in the eyes of his co-workers as they turned away from him, most likely grateful for the new topic of conversation.

"Sir," he heard Amy say to one of the men who had helped him up. "You came."

Noah looked to his side to see Chip Harington, smiling down awkwardly at him. He quickly remembered why he had spun around so quickly on his chair, and his cheeks burned crimson.

"Are you sure you're okay?" Clark asked, his hand rubbing the back of Noah's neck. "Maybe you should go and get checked out at the hospital?"

"Honestly, I'm fine." Noah shrugged away Clark's hand and blinked hard, unsure if he was concussed, or if the wine was resurfacing. "I just need to sit down."

"There's a VIP area upstairs," said Chip, to his surprise. "It'll be quieter."

Chip put his hand in the middle of Noah's back and led him away from Clark and Amy, and through the busy crowd. He glanced over his shoulder at Clark and Amy, who both looked visibly shocked, but he knew for different reasons.

They broke through the crowd and walked over to a spiralling metal staircase, which was closed off by a red rope. With the confidence only a man like Chip Harington could have, he unhooked the rope and stepped aside for Noah to walk up first. Each step made the embarrassment and shame of falling over in front of his boss grow even heavier.

The VIP area was a small room with its own bar, tucked away from the noise and hustle of the main area. The industrial theme from downstairs was continued throughout, but the bar was empty. When Noah sat down in one of the deep Chesterfield sofas, he was suddenly glad of the silence.

He watched as Chip jumped over the bar and started to look through the brightly lit fridges. He grabbed a glass bottle of water and vaulted back over the bar like a man who was dressed for the gym, and not wearing a full tuxedo. He was a far-cry away from the man Noah had left drinking whiskey in his office a couple of hours earlier.

"I'm so embarrassed," mumbled Noah as he accepted the water.

"Don't be," said Chip with a gentle laugh as he sat

down on the Chesterfield dangerously close to Noah. "I was dreading showing my face here, so your timing was perfect."

"Glad I could help," said Noah as he sipped his water again. "I bet they're never going to let me live this one down."

"I thought you were above idle office gossip," said Chip, an unexpected strength in his voice. "You'll be fine."

Noah nodded as he sipped his water again. Chip stretched out his arm across the back of the leather couch and Noah felt a metal cufflink brush against his neck.

"Clark was right about getting checked out," said Chip, turning his head to Noah, his breath letting Noah know that he had probably drained a lot of the whiskey left in the Jameson bottle. "You might not realise how bad it is because you've been drinking."

"It's fine," he said, lifting his hand to the back of his head again. "It hurts a little, but it's not cut, I don't think."

"Let me see," said Chip, suddenly twisting in his seat and sitting up straight.

Noah glanced cautiously at Chip before turning around and dropping his head. When Chip's fingers carefully probed his hair, brushing up against his tender scalp, he inhaled deeply as his stomach writhed. If he was in any pain, he was too distracted to feel it.

"It looks okay to me," said Chip, slapping Noah on the shoulder. "My diagnosis is that you'll live."

"Thanks, Dr. Chip," Noah joked as he turned back and resumed sipping his water. "That free bar is dangerous."

"I guess I'll take the blame for this one." Chip held up his hands. "I just wanted you guys to have fun."

"I think the fun is over for me. My bed is calling."

"Are you sure?" asked Chip, his brow furrowing. "I'd hate to think I've ruined your night."

"Why would you think that?"

"Why else were you spinning around so quickly that you fell?" he said with a knowing smile as he arched a brow. "Nobody expected me to show up tonight."

"I hoped you might."

"Really?"

"I didn't think you would."

"I almost didn't," Chip sighed and stretched his hand out over the back of the couch again, his metal cufflink resting even harder against Noah's neck. "Especially after what happened today. Sasha showing up just got everybody talking about me. I didn't want an entire night of sympathetic looks and awkward conversation."

"What made you change your mind?"

"I realised not showing up would probably do more harm than *showing* up." Chip stared ahead at the bar, his eyes glazing over slightly. “Christmas isn’t a time for drinking whiskey alone in your office.”

For a moment, Noah wondered if what he had said to Chip had made a difference in him showing up. He shrugged off the thought, knowing his opinion probably didn’t sway his boss one way or another. Chip Harington was a strong man with a will of steel, much like his father, or so people said. By the time Noah had joined the company, Frank Harington had long since died and Chip had taken over.

“I’m sure they’re glad you came,” said Noah. “Despite what you might think, people like you.”

“Doesn’t mean they’re not talking about me, though, does it?”

Noah didn’t answer. For some reason, he couldn’t bring himself to lie. Forgetting Chip’s arm was behind him, he rolled his head back, but he quickly sat back upright when he felt Chip’s palm touching his red hair.

“I looked over your revisions,” said Chip, suddenly changing the gears of the conversation. “You did a really good job.”

“Are you sure that’s not the whiskey talking?” he joked.

“You always do a good job,” said Chip, grabbing the back of Noah’s neck, just like Clark had done, but without making him feel like he wanted to run away. “I know I can always depend on you, Noah.”

Noah couldn't help but smile. It didn't matter that he had a crush on his boss, he knew he was a great businessman and being complimented on his work by Chip meant a lot to him. He turned to Chip to thank him, but when he saw Chip smiling back, he couldn't bring himself to speak.

He parted his lips, but they closed just as quickly. Chip's dark eyes darted down to Noah's lips. Noah had never been able to read those eyes, but his wine goggles were trying their best to. Were they telling him that he wanted to kiss Noah?

Not waiting around to figure it out, Noah leaned in and pressed his lips softly against Chip's. Whether from sheer shock or pity, Chip's lips met Noah's with such tenderness, it made Noah snap out of it and realise what he was doing.

As quickly as he had dived in, Noah pulled away and rested his head in his hands.

"I'm so sorry," he said. "It's the wine, or the concussion, or – *I should go.*"

Unable to look at his boss, he headed straight for the staircase, wondering what the hell he had done. He hadn't expected Chip to follow him, so when thick fingers closed around his wrist, he stopped in his tracks and turned around.

"Noah, wait," said Chip, his lips still glistening from Noah's attempted kiss. "Let me drive you. There's Christmas parties all over the city so you'll never get a taxi."

"You've been drinking."

"My driver is parked out front," said Chip with a smile so friendly and soft, it made Noah feel pathetic for trying to kiss the man who would forgive his recklessness so easily.

"It's okay," said Noah, pulling away from Chip's grip. "You've only just arrived."

"I only came to show my face," he called after Noah. "I told the driver to keep the engine running."

Standing at the top of the spiralling staircase, Noah looked down into the party. He spotted Amy, back with Steve in the dark corner. He also spotted Clark, who was flirting with a guy he didn't recognise at the bar. He noticed Clark's hand on the man's thigh and he turned back to face Chip.

"Is there a backdoor out of this place?" Noah asked.

Chip smirked and jerked his head along the balcony framing the upper-level of the bar. With no clue what was going on, Noah followed Chip along the balcony, down a second staircase and through an emergency fire exit into the dark alley next to the club.

As he climbed into the backseat of the heated car, he allowed himself a moment of madness to imagine his fantasies coming true, but he resigned himself to the fact that his boss was taking pity on him.

CHAPTER *Four*

When Chip's car pulled up outside of Noah's block of flats, he was sad that the journey was over. They hadn't talked about much, but he had always found it surprisingly easy to be in the company of the man who employed him.

"This is me," said Noah, looking up at his modern block of flats in a new development in London's East End, feeling remarkably more sober than when they'd set off.

"It's nice," said Chip. "London's not an easy place

to buy."

Noah nodded his agreement, not wanting to let on that he was renting. When he had turned twenty, it had been in his ten-year plan to own a house by the age of twenty-six, and now that he was twenty-six, he wasn't sure if he was going to have the deposit for a mortgage saved up before the end of his next ten-year plan.

"Don't go to sleep straight away," said Chip.

"Huh?"

"In case of concussion."

"Oh." Noah laughed. "Right."

"That'll be the concussion," Chip said with a playful wink.

It had been twenty minutes since Noah had tried to kiss Chip, and his boss wasn't making him suffer for it. Noah doubted Chip would ever bring it up again. He still could not believe that he had somehow managed to kiss the man he had had a crush on for two full years. If that was all he would get to have, it was enough to send him to sleep.

With his hand on the door handle, he looked up at his flat, where the lights were still on from before he had left. He hadn't expected to be home before midnight, nor had he expected to spend the night alone. With the stark reality facing him that he was going to be spending the next five days off work and completely alone in his flat, he suddenly turned to

Chip, allowing himself one more minute of madness.

"Do you want to come up for some coffee?" Noah asked, unsuccessfully hiding the nerves in his voice. "I might even have some whiskey in the back of the cupboard from my last house party."

Noah caught Chip catching eyes with the driver in the rear view mirror. For a moment, and to Noah's complete surprise, he looked like he was considering accepting the invitation. Just when Noah let himself get excited, Chip shook his head and looked down into his lap.

"I should get going," he said quietly. "I've already stayed out longer than I expected to."

Noah didn't fight it. He smiled one last time and pulled on the door handle. Stepping out of the car, the cold nipped at his skin, and despite the forecast saying otherwise, soft white flakes of snow were starting to flutter on the wind.

Deciding it would be easier not to look back, he set off across the courtyard towards his flat's door, pulling his keys from his pocket. He was sure in the morning he was going to wake up with a sore head, full of shame and embarrassment for his three major missteps, but tonight, the fall, the kiss and the invitation didn't feel like such heavy weights on his mind.

Before he punched in the security code on his door's keypad, he pulled up the sleeve of his shirt and checked his watch. Its face was cracked and the hands were frozen, no doubt from his fall. Sighing, he shook the watch next to his ear. He didn't know what time it was, but he hoped it was before midnight so he could run to the local supermarket before it closed for Christmas Eve.

"It's half-past eleven," a familiar voice called from behind him.

Noah turned to see Chip walking through the softly falling snow, wearing a heavy, black trench coat he hadn't been wearing in the car, it's collar popped and protecting him from the cold.

"Chip?"

"I told Mike to get off home," said Chip calmly and casually. "He's got kids and I live all the way across London."

"Like you said, getting a taxi will be hard tonight."

"Is that offer of coffee not on the table anymore?" he chuckled.

"Oh." Noah shook his head, wondering if he was concussed after all. "I was just about to go and grab some wine."

"Coffee will be okay for me," said Chip, reaching into his inside pocket and pulling out a small, silver hipflask. "I always have this."

After struggling with the key in his tricky lock, Noah fell into his messy flat, completely embarrassed that he was having company with it being in such a state. Having his best friend inside was one thing, but his boss was a whole different level.

"Sorry about the mess," said Noah as he stacked up plates on the counter and dumped them in the sink. "It's easy to be messy when you live alone."

"Sasha was always a clean freak," he said as he shrugged off his coat. "It's nice seeing somewhere that's lived in."

Noah wasn't sure if Chip was being sincere with his words, but he didn't seem to be casting a judgemental eye around his flat, although his eyes did pause on the bleak Christmas tree balancing on a magazine on a small side table.

"I wasn't really planning on doing Christmas this year," said Noah apologetically. "I bought that thing last minute."

Noah quickly collected up the clothes off the couch and stuffed them in the washing machine, despite most of them still being clean. When he started to collect the books, DVDs and empty mugs off his coffee table, he felt like he was putting a Band-Aid over a gaping wound.

"You don't have to tidy up on my account," said Chip as he tossed his jacket over the back of the couch. "It's fine as it is."

Noah quickly stuffed the books and DVDs back on the bookshelf and dropped the mugs in the sink along with the plates before calming down. He watched as Chip stood at the double glass doors, which led out onto his small balcony.

"You've got a good view of London up here," Chip remarked as he unscrewed the cap of his hipflask.

Noah almost mentioned that Chip's view was probably nicer, when he remembered the divorce and the likelihood that Chip had been sleeping on his couch in his office for weeks. He watched Chip's reflection in the dark window, as he sipped from his hipflask to the backdrop of falling snow.

Deciding coffee was the best option for his head, Noah quickly washed two mugs and filled up the kettle. He scooped generous heaps of coffee and sugar into the mugs, before adding a splash of milk, and the boiled water. When he walked back through to the living room area of his tiny, open-plan flat, Chip was sitting comfortably in the corner of Noah's couch. Noah set the two coffees on the small table, trying not to analyse how or why his impossibly handsome boss was sitting in his flat the day before Christmas Eve.

Before he sat down, he flicked on a small digital radio and set the Christmas pop songs to a level that suited as background noise for a conversation.

"This is good coffee," said Chip as he sipped from the rim of the mug.

"It's just instant," replied Noah, almost defensively.

"It's better than the stuff in the machines at the office."

"Tell me about it!" Noah sighed. "That stuff tastes like piss water – I mean –"

Chip laughed and shook his head. He took another sip of the coffee, before leaning forward to put it on the table next to Noah's. With one tug, he unclipped his bow tie, unbuttoned his collar and let the two hang loose at his neck.

"You don't have to apologise for being honest," said Chip as he stretched out his arm over the back of the couch. "I'm not your boss tonight."

"Yes, sir."

"Chip."

"Right."

"Let's call it the concussion," said Chip with a flash of his pearly white grin.

Noah reached out to pick up his mug but his fingers completely missed the handle and he sent the mug with the coffee tumbling to the floor.

"*Shit!*" he cried, jumping up.

"Concussion?" chuckled Chip.

"I wish," sighed Noah as he hurried through to the kitchen to grab a cloth. "My Granddad always used to say that I was born with two left hands and two left feet."

Noah hurried back into the living room with a yellow cloth, where Chip was on the floor, picking up the broken fragments of Noah's favourite two-coffee wide mug. Noah bent down to mop up the coffee from the laminated wood floor, but Chip took the cloth and mopped up the coffee puddle for him.

"After tonight, I think I'll have to agree with your Granddad," said Chip. "Thankfully, you're a better contract writer than you are a functioning human being."

"I'll take that as a compliment."

"I meant it as one."

They caught each other's eyes for a second and shared a quick smile. When they both went to stand up, they bumped heads, but before Noah could apologise again, Chip waved his hand and laughed. Noah tossed the cloth back into the kitchen and resumed his place on the couch. Instead of sitting in the opposite corner, Chip opted to sit in the middle, directly next to Noah.

"You're a bit of a mystery, aren't you Noah?" said Chip as he rested his head on the headrest.

"Why do you say that?"

"Because you're the first person to speak to me for more than a couple of minutes and not ask me about my divorce."

"It's none of my business," he said quietly, also leaning his head on the headrest. "It's nobody's business but yours."

Chip smiled for a moment before turning his head

away to look out of the window. The snow was falling thick and fast, and Noah imagined Amy standing outside the bar, shivering and smoking a cigarette with Steve latched to her neck. She probably hadn't noticed he had left.

"I brought it on myself." The vulnerability in Chip's voice took Noah by surprise, making him lean in to listen closer. "I should have done what I knew was right, not what I thought was right."

Noah thought about what he meant, but the metaphor didn't click. He thought about what Beth had said about Chip cheating on his wife, but even now, he couldn't believe that was true.

"Relationships aren't easy," said Noah. "Nobody knows how they work. We just make it up."

"Have you ever been close to being married?" Chip asked, turning back to Noah. "I don't think I've ever heard you talk about a man."

Noah had never outwardly told his boss that he was gay, but if the drunken mess of a kiss didn't confirm it, it must have been obvious somehow.

"There've been a couple of men, but nobody has ever stuck," said Noah, thinking back to his last serious relationship with Jackson, four years ago, before Jackson moved to northern England, leaving Noah behind in London.

"Why's that?"

"I don't know," he frowned, trying to think why.

"I guess I've never met the right person. I don't think you can have your heart broken if you've never been in love."

"You've never been in love?" Chip asked, visibly surprised.

Noah was surprised by his own admission too. He had never vocally admitted that he had never found the one, but it was something he had thought about in the back of his mind late at night when he was feeling lonely.

"I don't think so."

"You'd know if you had been," sighed Chip, his eyes darting down and glazing over for a second.

Noah almost asked if Chip had been in love with his recent wife, Sasha, but he stopped himself. From the tears streaking down Sasha's face and the lack of tears in Chip's eyes, he knew who had broken whose heart.

"My Granddad always used to tell me I would know love when it hit me, and until it did, I should just sit tight and wait," said Noah.

"Your Granddad sounds like a very wise man."

"He was," said Noah, a lump catching in his throat. "He died early in the year."

"Oh," Chip frowned. "I'm sorry. I had no idea."

"It's okay. I didn't tell anyone. Well, I told Amy, but I tell her everything."

"Didn't you take some time off work?"

"I took that holiday, didn't I?"

"You told me you were going to Italy on a last minute city break," Chip shook his head. "Were you worried I wouldn't give you compassionate leave? I'm not a monster, Noah."

"I know you're not," he said quickly. "You're a great boss, I just didn't want people knowing. I didn't want to have people asking if I was okay all the time. I just wanted to deal with it in my own time. He was all I had."

Chip grabbed his hipflask from his inside pocket and offered it to Noah. He didn't think twice before grabbing it and taking a deep sip.

"You must have somebody else," said Chip softly. "Everybody has somebody."

"I have Amy," he nodded. "But no other family. My mum didn't know who my dad was and she died when I was young. I don't really remember her, and my Granddad was my only other family, so he raised me. It was just me and him."

"That must be hard."

Noah took another sip of the whiskey, trying his best not to cry. He still had Christmas to get through, and he didn't want to shed any unnecessary tears.

"My mum lives in Spain," offered Chip. "I never really see her much. I have a brother, but he's in the Army and he lives up North with his wife and kids. My dad died eight years ago, and that's when I took over Harington Publishing House."

"And you're doing a great job," said Noah, tipping the flask up to Chip before taking another sip and handing it back.

"You think?" he said with a sarcastic laugh. "My cheap gossip overshadows the work every time something like this happens, and there's so much more to come."

"More?"

"So much more," he said through a strained smile. "Now that it's out there, it won't take long until the word gets around. You'll understand."

"I will?"

"How did you come out?"

"Come out?" Noah choked on the words. "Why?"

Chip laughed, his brow furrowing. Was Noah missing something completely obvious?

"It took three failed marriages for me to finally say it out loud, but I guess it's better late than never. I just wish I hadn't put those women through it."

Noah took the hipflask from Chip's hands and took a deep gulp. The whiskey burned his stomach and softened his mind. He wiped his mouth with the back of his hand before passing the hipflask back.

"Are you trying to tell me you're gay, Chip?" asked Noah, almost not believing the words that were coming from his mouth.

"I thought we'd established that already?" He said,

arching a dark brow high up his forehead. "I kissed you."

"*I* kissed *you*!" Noah corrected him.

"Because I thought I made it obvious that I wanted you to?"

Noah suddenly stood up, his mind swimming. He walked over to the double doors and yanked them open. The cold night air hit him like a bath of cold water, but it was just the shock he needed. He looked up at the sky and let the snow flutter down onto his pale skin.

"Noah, it's freezing," said Chip, appearing behind him.

"I just needed some fresh air."

"Is it that much of a shock to you?" Chip laughed.

"Yes!"

"I always thought you knew, because you're the same."

"It doesn't work like that," said Noah, turning around to face Chip. "Are you sure?"

"I'm thirty-two, and I've been married three times, hoping every new woman would change things for me. I'm sure."

"But are you sure you're sure?"

Chip laughed and shook his head, clearly confused by Noah's ramblings. Maybe he was concussed after all?

Noah clenched his eyes shut, daring to test his

theory. The cold felt too bitter not to be real, but he expected to open his eyes and be on the floor in the bar, with a crowd of people looking over him.

When he opened them, he saw Chip's amused and confused smile.

Noah didn't second-guess his next move. Wrapping his fingers around Chip's shirt, he pulled his boss in and their lips collided.

CHAPTER *Five*

They stumbled and fell through Noah's flat as they made their way to his bedroom, their lips never breaking contact. Chip opened wide to Noah and they explored each other's mouths as their hands frantically explored each other's bodies.

When he finally felt his bedroom door behind his back, Noah twisted the handle and kicked it open. He fell backwards onto his unmade bed, with Chip on top of him. He considered that the possibility of him being in a concussion-induced dream was still very real, but it felt too good to care. He had had sex dreams about his boss before, but nothing had felt as real as the man on top of him.

Chip rolled onto his back, pulling Noah on top of him. Heavy fingers tugged at the buttons of Noah's shirt, ripping them clean off. Noah didn't care that it was his most expensive and favourite shirt. He could buy a new one, but he probably would never get another chance to have Chip willing and in his bedroom.

Noah broke the kiss for a moment to yank off the remains of his shirt. Chip smiled up at him, his dark eyes drinking in every inch of Noah's toned, milky torso. Chip grabbed a fistful of Noah's hair, dragging him down into another kiss.

Something hard pulsed against Noah, forcing him to kiss Chip even deeper. With fumbling fingers, Noah worked on unbuttoning Chip's shirt, but Chip brushed his fingers away, and ripped it open, as he had done to Noah's. Sitting upright for a moment, Noah stared down at Chip's lightly haired and perfectly sculpted chest. Instead of re-joining Chip's lips, he pressed his lips hard against the contours of Chip's chiselled stomach. A small moan escaped Chip's throat as he tightened his grip on Noah's red hair, pushing him further down.

Noah kissed above Chip's belt buckle as his boss worked on unfastening it. Within seconds, he was ripping his trousers open, leaving Noah to peel back his tight, white underwear.

His solid cock bounced up onto Chip's stomach, begging to be touched. Noah took a moment to admire it, disbelieving what he was about to do. He was grateful for the whiskey washing around in his mind, because his doubts and inhibitions weren't with him tonight.

After yanking Chip's underwear and trousers down his thick thighs, Noah straddled him and dived in to run his tongue along Chip's meaty cock. It twitched, pleading with Noah to take it into his mouth; Noah obliged.

He took his boss's length deep into his throat, encouraged by Chip's forceful hand on the back of his head. Breathing through his nose, he looked up into Chip's eyes, who was already looking into his. Noah's stomach knotted, and knotted again, until it felt so small and tight, all he could do was moan.

Gripping his fingers around the thick base of Chip's shaft, he worked it, knowing he was messy, but being too intoxicated by the moment to care. If Chip didn't like it, his moans and encouraging hand were deceiving.

Using his hair like a handle, Chip pulled Noah back up his body, and back to his lips. They kissed deeply, Chip seeming to enjoy the taste of himself on Noah's tongue. Before Noah could ask where things were going, Chip's fingers unfastened Noah's belt and freed his cock.

"Have you –,"

"Yeah."

Reluctantly, Noah got off of Chip and hurried over to his bedside drawer. He picked up a small, silver packet, and a bigger blue sachet, kicked off his trousers and hurried back to kissing Chip.

Without breaking the kiss, Noah ripped open the silver packet and rolled the rubber down Chip's cock. He ripped open the sachet and slathered the cold lube on Chip's waiting shaft. Chip inhaled sharply and laughed through the kiss.

"Are you sure about this?" Noah found himself asking.

"Aren't you?"

"Do I even need to answer that?"

Noah pushed his tongue deep into Chip's mouth as he guided Chip's cock in between his cheeks. The cold jelly hit him and he let out a small gasp; a mixture of excitement and fear.

Inch by inch, he took Chip into him, guiding him the whole way. He realised he was completely in control, so he started off slow, bucking his hips gently up and down Chip's shaft.

Chip wrapped his arms around Noah's shoulders, pulling him in tightly. Chip kissed his chest, his tongue exploring each nipple as Noah found his rhythm. It was unlike anything Noah had felt before.

He had never felt so connected to the man who was fucking him.

To his surprise, Chip tightened his grip on Noah and rolled him over onto his back, not breaking their connection. Chip dragged Noah to the edge of the bed and Noah wrapped his legs around Chip's backside.

Diving in, Chip kissed Noah once more as he fucked him harder and deeper than anybody had dared to before. Noah cried out, moaning louder and louder, not caring if any, or if all of his neighbours, could hear him. He didn't care if the whole of London heard what he was doing tonight, because even he couldn't believe it was happening.

But it was happening. As he felt Chip's hips thrust against him, he tightened his thigh's grip around Chip's middle, making every muscle in his body tighten. Arching his back, he reached out his hand behind him, and grabbed the other edge of his shaking bed.

Chip tossed his head back, every muscle of his Adonis body glistening in sweat. His beautiful face was contorted, with screwed up eyes and mouth open, but still retaining its impossible beauty.

Noah thought about the boss he had lusted over for two years, forcing his eyes to stay open and absorb every inch of what was happening. He suddenly wished his mind was free from the influence of alcohol, so he could remember and savour every glorious detail of the act.

Chip dived in once more, joining their lips and silencing Noah's thoughts. Chip's stomach rubbed against Noah's own cock, edging him closer and closer to that sweet spot. When he thought he was about to blow, Chip whispered that he was close and he arched his back.

Grabbing Noah's legs and using them like handles, he sped up, grunting and panting with each thrust. Just when Noah thought Chip had forgotten about him, Chip's fingers closed in around his shaft, and they quickly raced to the brink of no return together.

Noah tried to force his eyes to stay open, but it was impossible. Whether it was the alcohol, the concussion, or the fact it was Chip, Noah didn't know, but when he finally gave into the feeling, he lost all control of his mind and body.

He knew he was crying out, but he couldn't hear it. He stared up at the dark ceiling, but static fuzz, which spread through his body at the speed of lightening, blinded him.

A sharp ringing in his ears brought him back down to reality and as Chip crashed down onto the bed next to him, Noah's mind landed back in his body. Staring into the darkness, he tried to think of the perfect thing to say, but he couldn't muster anything. He heard Chip snap off the condom and toss it on the nightstand, but the only other sound filling the silence was their frantic panting for breath.

Noah wondered if Chip regretted what they had just done, but before he could analyse it anymore, his mind slipped into the darkness and the world around him faded away.

CHAPTER
Six

The cold woke Noah up. Naked and shivering, he shot up in bed, wondering why he had fallen asleep on top of the sheets. He rubbed his eyes and frozen nose as he crawled under the sheets.

In his sleepy haze, he rested his head on the pillow, happy to go back to sleep as he let the sheets thaw out his icy skin. Chip came into his mind and his eyes darted open, suddenly wide-awake. For a moment, he thought the whole thing had been a twisted dream, dragged up from the deep depths of his imagination; it wouldn't be the first time. When he noticed the condom on the nightstand, he knew it hadn't been.

Dragging himself out of bed, he crawled into the fluffy robe Amy had given him as an early Christmas present. He secured the tie around his waist as he scanned the floor for any more evidence of Chip.

Just when he was coming to the conclusion that Chip had fled his flat the second Noah had fallen asleep, he heard the tricky lock of his front door rattle. Noah stuffed his feet into his matching slippers and shuffled out to his hallway.

Chip turned around with an apologetic smile, not quite meeting Noah's eyes. He had one hand on the door handle, which he had managed to open, and the other clutching his phone. Noah half expected Chip to slip out without so much as an explanation, but to his surprise, he softly closed the door and turned to face him.

"Morning," said Chip, rather awkwardly.

"Morning," replied Noah, his vocal chords grating from the sub-zero temperatures in his flat. "Coffee?"

Five minutes later, the radiators were firing up with a loud rattle, and he was pouring boiling hot water into two mugs. They sat across from each other at the breakfast bar, hugging their mugs, while talking casually about the weather. After his first sip of coffee, the memory of falling over in the bar burned brightly in his mind, causing his hand to raise to the back of his head. Through his thick, ginger hair, his fingertips brushed up against the tiny bump.

"You should probably get that checked out," said Chip quite seriously as he blew the surface of his coffee. "Does it hurt?"

"The embarrassment does."

Chip laughed and sipped his coffee. Noah felt the awkwardness melt a little, just as he started to feel warmth seeping from the radiators.

"You have nothing to feel embarrassed about," said Chip. "We've all been there."

"I doubt you've been on your arse in a bar in front of all of your colleagues," mumbled Noah, feeling his pale cheeks redden. "I'm never going to live that one down."

"You made it a night to remember," he said with a smirk. "You never remember the nights nothing happened and you went to sleep early."

Noah thought about Chip's words for a moment, wondering if he was talking about his fall in the bar, or what had happened when they got back to his flat. When he had invited Chip up to his flat for coffee, he hadn't expected anything to come of it. The thought that they would end up in bed together was the last thing he expected, which made Chip's attempt at an early morning escape sting even more. Noah almost didn't ask about it, but he knew the question would burn a hole in his mind all day.

"Ah," said Chip, placing his coffee on the counter as he absorbed Noah's question. "I suppose I should explain."

"I mean, you don't have to," said Noah, trying to shrug it off. "It wouldn't be the first time I'd woken up alone after a night like that."

Noah almost regretted the words as soon as they had come out of his mouth. If he was being honest with himself, he had never had a night like that before. He had had one-night stands, just like everybody else his age, but nothing like that.

"It wasn't like that," said Chip, rather darkly. "It's Christmas Eve, I didn't want to complicate things for you."

Noah stared into his coffee. Aside from the chill still nipping the tops of his ears, he had forgotten all about the looming holiday.

"There's nothing to complicate. It's not like I have any grand plans for Christmas."

"I just thought I should get home and get out of your hair," said Chip, picking up his coffee again. "I wasn't expecting last night to happen."

Chip's lie caught Noah off guard. Chip didn't know that Noah knew he was sleeping in his office. For a moment, he wondered if he had been wrong about that. He knew a sleeping bag in his office didn't mean he was sleeping there permanently, but it seemed very likely. He decided not to confront Chip, so he took a deep sip of his coffee, and waited for his boss to speak again.

"I should get going," said Chip. "Thanks for the coffee."

Noah tried to offer Chip breakfast but he politely declined. The passion and the fire from the night before had been dampened, and it almost felt like they were employee and employer again. Noah was already dreading his return to work in the new year.

After an awkward moment at the door where Noah thought Chip was going to kiss him, but didn't, Chip vanished down the stairwell without a second look in Noah's direction, leaving Noah to stand in his doorway, feeling completely confused by what had happened.

He didn't know how long he stood there, but when he heard his neighbours across the hallway unlocking their door, he retreated into his flat and locked the door. Leaning against the wood, he stared down his cluttered hallway and into the kitchen, where the two coffee mugs were still sitting on his counter.

Noah did the only thing he knew to do. He grabbed his phone, and he called Amy.

Two hours later, Noah walked through the busy streets of London, dodging last minute shoppers, while getting his shoes wet from the previous night's melting snow.

Pulling his scarf tighter around his neck, he approached the café, already spotting Amy hugging a large mug of hot chocolate in a sofa facing the window. From the way she stared right through him, it was obvious she was feeling a little worse for wear after last night's antics.

Noah unraveled his thick layers, grabbed a coffee and collapsed next to Amy on the plush sofa.

"How're you feeling?" he asked.

"Sore," she mumbled. "Sore and rough."

"Sore?" he asked, arching a brow as he sipped his hot coffee.

A playful smirk tickled her lips, which were still stained with last night's lipstick. Noah didn't need to ask anymore.

"I wasn't expecting Steve to be so big," she said, shifting uncomfortably in her seat.

"I'm guessing you had sex last night?"

"In his bedroom, in his kitchen, in his bathroom," she said, her smirk growing. "Jesus, he was good. My pussy is killing me."

"*Bloody hell*, Amy," he said, spitting his coffee back into his mug. "Too much information."

"You're gay," she said, shrugging and settling further into the sofa. "To be honest with you, I haven't slept. I came straight from Steve's place. I think I'm still drunk. Had to put a splash of brandy in this to feel alive. Want some?"

After a quick glance in the direction of the counter, she pulled a silver hipflask from her clutch, reminding him why he had asked to meet her in the first place.

"No thanks," he said, putting his hand over his cup. "I'm only just starting to feel alive. It's taken four cups of coffee, but I'm getting there."

"It's called hair of the dog!" she said in a matter-of-fact voice. "It's just a little pick me up. Gets you drunk enough to not have a come down."

"Isn't that just a delayed hangover?"

"Whatever," she said with another shrug. "I'll just crash before I set off for my Gran's house. I don't have to be there until six. Why do you need coffee to feel alive? Don't think I didn't notice you slipping off early last night! I asked around and nobody saw you after you death dropped off your chair."

Noah buried his face in his mug. He took a deep sip of the hot coffee, hoping it would explain why his cheeks were blushing. He was stuck somewhere between wanting to tell Amy everything, and wanting to keep it a secret a little longer. A smile tickled his lips and he knew he couldn't keep it in for much longer.

"You had sex last night!" Amy exclaimed a little too loudly for Noah's liking. "I thought I could smell it on you."

Noah took a sniff of his shirt, unsure if Amy was joking or not. He glanced around the coffee shop, hoping the hustle and bustle of Christmas Eve shoppers had drowned out her declaration.

"So, who was he?" she teased. "Was it Clark? He didn't stick around too long after you ditched him to talk with the boss."

"It wasn't Clark," he said, avoiding her eyes.

"Tim?" she asked, her eyes narrowing. "Please tell me it wasn't Tim."

"Me and Tim have never had sex," he said, almost offended. "You know he's a complete whore."

"Don't insult my people," she joked, jabbing him in the ribs. "*Come on*! Spill the beans! I want every detail. Ugh, it wasn't Jackson was it? He didn't move back to London after his great escape up North? Please tell me you haven't touched that slime."

"It wasn't Jackson."

"Thank God," she said, letting out a sigh of relief. "Noah, spit it out! Is it somebody I know?"

Noah turned to the steamed up window, squinted through the twinkling lights lining the frame, and through the crowd of shoppers, to Harington Publishing House across the road. He had expected Amy to question why he had asked to meet her in the coffee shop directly across from their work, but she seemed too distracted to notice.

"You know him, alright," he mumbled.

"Is he ugly? Is that why you don't want to say?"

Noah laughed and sipped his coffee. Chip

Harington was as far from 'ugly' as a man could get. Even Amy agreed he was the most beautiful man she had ever seen. Noah inhaled deeply, knowing he couldn't drag it out any longer. Exhaling shakily, he turned to Amy, and set his mug on the coffee table in front of them.

"It was Chip."

Amy choked on her brandy tainted hot chocolate. Her eyes popped out of her head as she coughed loudly into her fist. Noah patted her on the back, almost embarrassed by her reaction. When her throat cleared, she frowned at Noah for a moment, before her mouth twisted into a smirk and she started laughing.

"Good one," she cried through the laughter as she wiped a tear from the corner of her eye. "You got me good there. Classic."

"I'm not joking."

"Chip?" she mocked. "Chip Harington? Our boss, Chip Harington? The same Chip Harington you have had a crush on since your first day working at Harington Publishing House? Chip?"

"Chip."

"Chip?"

"Chip!" he said through pursed lips. "I'm not lying!"

Amy squinted at him, staring deep into his eyes. Noah didn't break her gaze, and when it became obvious that he wasn't lying to the only woman who would be able to tell, her eyes widened again. This time, she reached into her handbag, pulled out her hipflask, and took a deep swig of brandy, not even caring if any of the baristas saw her. When she offered the hipflask to Noah this time, he accepted.

After wiping away the brandy from his lips, he started at the beginning and told Amy everything. She hung on to every word without interruption. When he finished, he let himself smile, because saying it all out loud only confirmed how excited he felt about it.

"Fucking hell, Noah," she said, shaking her head and glancing across the road to the building they worked in. "I'm speechless. Absolutely fucking speechless. It's like – It's like a Christmas miracle!"

"Not quite," he interrupted. "Did you miss the part where he couldn't wait to get out of my flat this morning? He's probably still in the shower trying to scrub my smell off him."

"Don't be stupid," she said, slapping him on the arm and rolling her eyes. "You're a catch. You're the second cutest guy I know, behind Steve, of course."

"Thanks, I guess?"

"What I'm trying to say is, Chip Harington is lucky to have had sex with you! It's not like you let many men into your fairy cave."

"I've asked you to stop saying that," he said, pursing his lips.

"Only when you stop referring to my pussy as a

'*vagina*'," she said with a playful wink. "It sounds so – medical! What happens now?"

"Nothing happens now," he said, looking over to Harington Publishing House again. "He left and he said he had to get home."

"But you think he's sleeping in his office?"

"I *know* he is," he mumbled. "I can feel it. He was lying."

Amy picked up her hot chocolate again and drained the last of the chocolate syrup lingering in the bottom of her mug, letting him know their meeting was about to be cut short.

"Maybe he's too proud to admit the truth," she said as she stood up, wrapping her chunky knitted, bright yellow scarf around her neck. "Divorce isn't easy. Look at my parents. Twenty years later and they still can't bear to be in the same room as each other. On top of that, he's been gay this whole time. That's the part that's baffled me the most. He seemed so – so straight!"

"There's no such thing these days," said Noah, as he joined Amy in pulling on his scarf and coat.

After Noah finished the last of his coffee, they walked out into the bustling street and they joined the rushing crowd. They headed to the end of the street, to the entrance to the tube station.

Before Noah descended below the street, he glanced back at Harington Publishing House, just as the light in Chip's office turned on.

CHAPTER
Seven

Noah twirled his Granddad's pipe between his fingers, thinking back to last Christmas. The cancer had taken most of his Granddad's mind by that point, so it hadn't been a very fun Christmas at Springhill Nursing Home. Shaking those thoughts to the back of his mind, he forced himself to remember the man who had raised him, before his illness.

He had been a kind and loving man, with more tolerance and patience than any person Noah had ever met. He had always been accepting of Noah's sexuality, and he had never made him feel like he was different from anyone else. Whenever Noah found himself overwhelmed, he would think about what his Granddad would do.

Placing the pipe back in its special box, he knew exactly what his Granddad would tell him to do in this situation; he wouldn't rest, knowing that another man was about to spend Christmas alone in an office.

Glancing out of the window at the heavy falling snow as a rerun of *The Muppet's Christmas Carol* played on the TV, he wondered if it was possible he had gotten it wrong. He thought about what Chip had said about needing to go home. Had he said that as an excuse to get out of Noah's flat before Noah started talking about sex?

Noah sighed. He knew Chip wasn't like that. He barely knew the man, but he knew he was a good man. He had never seen him raise his voice or show his temper, even when Sasha was screaming in his face, belittling him in front of the entire office. Much like Noah's Granddad, Chip had a tolerance and patience that would make any man a fortune if he were able to bottle it.

His phone vibrated with a picture message from Amy. She was leaning on her hand, her mouth open mid-yawn, with a Christmas hat blending into her red hair. Smiling, he replied with: '*you're still having more fun than me*'. They had been texting on and off all day, and it was clear her shock had worn off because she had gone from asking questions about the sex, to asking questions about the future.

'*Are you even going to be able to work with him now?*' one of her messages had read. Noah hadn't thought that far ahead. Amy would be back for New Year's Eve and she would no doubt drag him out of his flat to see in the new year in some random, over-crowded bar in Soho, but when January rolled around, he would be back in his cubicle, watching Chip from across the office, just like he had done for two years. It didn't seem right, but that was the reality of the situation. It felt so far away, but he knew how quickly it would roll around.

He glanced at the TV, but he couldn't pay attention to The Muppets. All he could think about was Chip, sitting alone in his office. The more he thought about it, the less he cared about their encounter and its possible repercussions, and the more he cared about a man spending Christmas alone.

It was this thought that compelled him to pull off his pajamas and climb into his jeans, thickest woolly jumper, heaviest coat, warmest scarf and gloves, and sturdiest boots. Despite being wrapped up tighter than a Christmas present, he knew he wasn't prepared for the weather the moment he opened the door.

Since retreating to the warmth of his flat after his coffee date with Amy, he had watched the snowfall slowly increase throughout the rest of the day. From his seventh floor flat, he hadn't expected there to be enough snow on the ground to swallow up his boots to his ankles.

Holding onto the front door of his building, he stared ahead at the buried courtyard, the snow still falling thick and fast. He considered turning back, but he knew he couldn't. Stuffing his hands in his pockets, he set off across London.

The London Underground was already closed for Christmas, which meant he had an hour trek across London through the snow. He had walked to work many times, but never through a snowstorm. He thought about calling for a taxi, but the roads were deserted, and the line between the road and the pavement had vanished under the snow.

Noah had never seen London so quiet; he felt like he was walking through a ghost town. Aside from a couple of extremely brave cars, which were attempting to crawl along the snow, he didn't encounter any other sign of life.

When he turned onto the street where his work building was, he felt practically naked. The snow had stuck to, and soaked right through any clothes he was wearing, freezing his skin to the bone. Even under the heavy scarf, which was wrapped up tight under his eyes, he could feel his nose glowing brighter than Rudolph's.

Squinting up into the snow, he exhaled a frosty sigh of relief when he saw the warm glow of Chip's office light. He considered using his ID card to get straight into the building, but his stomach hurt from hunger, and he knew only alcohol would warm his bones.

He carefully trekked for another two streets, to a twenty-four-hour supermarket on one of London's many street corners. It was one of the few shops still open late on Christmas Eve and Noah didn't think he had ever been so grateful to see its luminous glow through the snow.

He pulled his scarf down his face and temporarily dragged his hat off his head. He ruffled his soaked hair as he grabbed a small shopping basket. First, he picked up two bottles of white wine, then three bags of his favourite salt and vinegar crisps, and a packet of microwave pizzas.

"You're brave," remarked the cashier girl when he handed over a damp twenty-pound note. "You're the first person we've had in since the snow got heavy. No idea how I'm getting home. Must be sharing this wine with somebody special if you're coming out in this."

"I hope so," he said as he bagged up his shopping and handed over an extra five-pound tip. "Merry Christmas."

The lift wasn't working so he climbed up the five flights of stairs to the top floor, where Chip's office was. On the way, he unravelled himself, layer by layer, so he was left in his woolly jumper and jeans; they were just as soaked through as his coat and scarf.

Unsure if he was sweating from the exercise or his nerves, he crossed the office and dumped his coat and scarf across the back of his chair. For a moment, he stood in his cubicle and stared across at Chip's office. The blinds were closed, but he saw the shadow of a man cross the window. He couldn't imagine sitting at his desk in the new year, pretending nothing had happened between them.

It suddenly struck him that Chip might be angry that Noah had taken it upon himself to turn up uninvited. He knew Chip hadn't mentioned that he was sleeping in his office out of pride, and Noah showing up out of the blue after piecing the jigsaw together could possibly whack a huge dent in that pride.

Knowing he had come too far to back out now, he brushed his damp hair, which had started to curl, out of his face, and he tightened his grip around the plastic bag. He looked inside at the wine bottles, wondering if it was too strong a gesture.

Trying not to make any noise, he crossed the office and paused outside of Chip's door. He lifted his fist but he didn't immediately strike the wood. He would never have thought about walking into his boss's office, but he had also never expected to end up in bed with the man. He unscrewed his fist and hovered over the handle, a dry lump forming in his throat.

He decided on knocking, but it was too late. The door opened, the light flooded the dark office, and Noah stumbled backwards just in time to miss the blow of Chip's baseball bat.

"Noah?" Chip cried, standing in the dark doorway in nothing more than a pair of tight, black briefs. "What the *hell* are you doing here?"

"Surprise," he mumbled sheepishly, holding out the plastic bag.

CHAPTER *Eight*

Chip helped Noah up off the floor and showed him into his office. It wasn't until Noah sat in front of the portable gas heater that he realised how cold he really was.

"You're shivering," said Chip as he dug through a black bag filled with his clothes. "Here, put these on."

Chip passed Noah a pair of grey sweatpants and a black t-shirt. Using his shaking fingers, he peeled off his damp clothes. He almost left on his Santa Claus briefs, but they were just as soaked as his jeans. He didn't know why he tried to hide his modesty with his hand, considering what they had done the night before, but he did anyway.

Chip pulled on a white t-shirt, which hugged each of his perfectly sculpted muscles, making it appear as though he had been poured into the fabric. Still in his contrasting black underwear, he sat on the sofa next to Noah, wrapped his arm around Noah's shoulder, and rubbed his cold arm gently.

"What are you doing here, Noah?" Chip whispered as Noah held his hands out to the glowing front of the heater.

"I could ask you the same thing," said Noah, attempting to laugh, but his voice trembled out of control.

Chip retracted his arm and leaned against his toned thighs. He clasped his hands together and rested them in front of his mouth, staring ahead at his desk with glazed eyes, looking like he had the weight of the world on his shoulders.

"Did you walk here?" Chip asked, avoiding the question. "Didn't you hear the weather warnings?"

"I was watching *The Muppet's Christmas Carol.*"

Chip peaked at Noah out of the side of his eyes, dropped his hands and chuckled softly. Noah returned the smile, his insides suddenly feeling a lot warmer.

"I love that film," Chip said softly. "How did you know I was here?"

Noah rubbed his hands together in the direction

of the heater, before retracting them and settling them in his lap. He leaned back in the sofa, glad the weight was off his feet. He took a moment to look around the office, which looked completely different from yesterday. Black bags filled with clothes scattered the room, toiletries, food and beer cluttered the desk, with a duvet and pillows rolled up underneath it. They were the objects of somebody planning to spend Christmas alone in an office block.

"I saw your sleeping bag yesterday," admitted Noah. "I didn't want to ask you about it, but when you said you were going home this morning, I knew you were lying."

Chip nodded and sucked the air through his teeth. Noah could tell he was embarrassed, but he didn't look as offended as Noah had expected.

"It technically wasn't a lie. This is my home at the moment," said Chip, his eyes glazing over again. "Sasha thinks I'm going to start burying money away before the divorce, so she managed to get the courts to freeze my savings accounts until the new year. There wasn't much I could do."

"Couldn't you have stayed in a hotel?"

"The only thing more depressing than spending Christmas alone in an office is spending Christmas alone with other people spending Christmas alone in a hotel," he said with a soft smile. "I don't think my ego could take the pitied looks of the staff."

Noah understood that. The only person who knew he was spending Christmas alone in his flat was Amy. He could have told more of his friends at work, and he knew it would have resulted in somebody insisting he spend Christmas with their family, but Noah didn't want the questions and the looks either.

"I was in London earlier today, with Amy. I saw the light from your office, so I knew you were here."

"And you came all this way to see if I was alright?"

"On foot."

"You're insane, Noah," said Chip, shaking his head. "Why would you do that?"

Noah thought for a moment. He wanted to ask questions about what their encounter meant for the future, but that wasn't the reason he trekked across London in the snow.

"I just didn't want you to be alone," said Noah after a moment's thought. "Some people aren't used to being alone."

Chip smiled gratefully before furrowing his brow and turning to face Noah.

"And you're used to being alone?" Chip asked him, his tone filled with concern.

"When I told you I didn't really have anybody, I wasn't lying," said Noah, inhaling deeply. "My Granddad was the only family I had."

"So you were going to spend Christmas alone too?"

Noah nodded.

"What you're saying is, you were okay spending Christmas alone, but you weren't okay with me spending Christmas alone?"

Noah thought about it for a moment before nodding again.

"That's very selfless of you," Chip said quietly. "There aren't many people like you around these days."

"Oh, I don't know. If you look hard enough, people aren't as bad as you think."

"Maybe you're right," said Chip with a nod. "What's in the bag?"

Noah suddenly remembered his last minute shopping trip. He picked up the plastic bag that was next to his damp clothes, and handed it over to Chip.

"Microwave pizzas, crisps, and wine?" Chip chuckled, as he peered in the bag.

"I think the cold got to my brain."

"I think you're right." Chip closed the bag and set it on the sofa between them. "What was your plan? Coming here, I mean. I'm guessing it wasn't to give me microwave pizzas and wine."

"I didn't think that far ahead," Noah admitted. "I just wanted to see if you were okay."

"I'm okay."

Noah nodded and he suddenly felt foolish. In the back of his mind, he had travelled all that way to take

Chip back to his flat with him, like a rescue puppy. With the snow as bad as it was, he couldn't expect Chip to walk back with him. He looked down at the bag as he felt the colour rush back into his face, in full force.

"I guess I'll get going then," said Noah, wiping his suddenly runny nose with the back of his hand.

He attempted to stand up, but Chip grabbed his wrist, just as he had done in the bar, and he pulled Noah back down onto the sofa. Noah looked down at Chip's fingers that were wrapped around his arm. He was sure his wrist was suddenly the hottest part of his body all of a sudden.

"You might be okay with spending Christmas alone, but I'm not okay with that," said Chip, letting go of Noah's wrist and resting his fingers on Noah's thigh. "As your boss, and your friend, I'm not okay with that."

Noah almost expected him to mention the sex from the night before, but he didn't. It almost felt like it hadn't happened.

"So you're suggesting I stay here?" asked Noah, looking around the office. "And spend Christmas here with you?"

"Why not?" Chip shrugged. "Even if you wanted to go back out there, I wouldn't let you. If you haven't come down with something after being out there for so long, you would do it all over again. As your boss, I'm ordering you to stay here, and I know you're not the type of employee who ignores his superior's orders."

Chip winked playfully at Noah, making him laugh. He was touched that Chip cared that much. Even if the sex was never mentioned again, Noah felt like he had gained a real friend.

"I guess I don't have a choice," said Noah.

"You don't."

"Looks like we're spending Christmas together."

"We are," said Chip, through what looked like a suppressed grin. "I might not be as good as *The Muppet's Christmas Carol*, but I'll try my hardest."

"I'm sure you will," said Noah, his stomach filling with butterflies. "I'm sure you will."

CHAPTER *Nine*

Noah shot up in his seat, clutching a ceramic mug full of white wine. Rubbing his eyes, he looked around the office, not remembering falling asleep. The gas heater was still roaring in front of him, keeping his legs toasty, but everything else looked different.

The fluorescent lights in the ceiling had been turned off, but the office wasn't in darkness. Twinkling fairy lights had been wrapped around anything that could be wrapped, bathing the room in a warm glow.

"What's all of this?" croaked Noah as he sat up properly, squinting into the low light at Chip behind his desk. "How long was I asleep?"

"You're awake," beamed Chip. "You were only out for about an hour."

"You did all of this in an hour?" Noah stood up and ran his fingers along the lights wrapped around a tall lamp next to the sofa.

"There was a spare box of those things in the stock room," he said, almost apologetically. "It's not too much, is it?"

"It's beautiful."

Noah spotted a cardboard cut-out of a Christmas tree wrapped in the lights, which was propped up against a filing cabinet.

"Another stock room find," said Chip, jumping up excitedly from his chair, still in his underwear. "Remember Tommy Sutcliffe's failed Christmas novel a couple of years ago? Still had a bunch of these from the launch."

"The one about the serial killer Santa Claus?" Noah squinted through the lights, noticing the blood splatters on the snow-covered pine needles.

"Why I thought that would work, I will never know," said Chip, rolling his eyes. "Oh, there's something else too!"

Chip wrapped his hand around Noah's and led him out of the warm office. Noah expected the rest of the building to be freezing cold again, but it seemed Chip had turned on the heating. He let Chip lead him through the boardroom and into a small kitchen, reserved for the board of directors.

When they were inside, Chip let go of Noah's hand and walked over to a double-fronted fridge. He tossed the doors open, revealing more champagne and food than Noah knew what to do with.

"We had a Christmas party for the directors during your lunch hour yesterday," said Chip. "We kept it a secret so the rest of the team wouldn't get jealous. There's plenty in here to throw together some kind of Christmas dinner tomorrow."

"So much for microwave pizzas," mumbled Noah as he peeled back the foil on a half-eaten turkey. "This is amazing."

An infectious childlike excitement Noah had never seen from his boss radiated from Chip. Noah couldn't help but smile.

"Just because we're stuck here, it doesn't mean we can't do things properly," said Chip as he carefully closed the fridge doors.

"How's the snow?"

"Let's go and have a look," said Chip, his grin widening. "Have you ever been up to the roof?"

Noah shook his head, so Chip held out his hand. Noah took it without a second thought and he let Chip take him back through the boardroom. He dug his nails into his palm, wondering how things could suddenly be so perfect.

Noah stood outside of the locked door leading up to the roof, which had a huge '*STRICTLY NO ACCESS*' sign plastered across it. He pulled the dry scarf from the lost property box around his neck, and fastened the lost property coat. It was a little big on him, but unlike his own coat, which was still hanging over the back of his chair soaked through, this one was waterproof.

"Don't laugh," Chip called from the stock room. "There wasn't much of a choice."

Chip walked out of the stock room, in a long, black trench coat, with a bright yellow scarf wrapped around his neck, purple gloves, and a pink hat covering his dark hair. Noah put his own gloved hand over his mouth, supressing a laugh, while wondering how Chip could still look so masculine in such hideous colours.

"It's a look," said Noah, giving into his urge to laugh.

"We never speak of this again," commanded Chip, as he pulled a bundle of keys from his pocket. "Thank God I turned the security cameras off last night. The directors would have a field day with this."

Chip rattled the key in the lock and the door swung open. Cold air blew down the stairwell, despite there being another door at the top of the dark corridor. Noah followed Chip up the dark, narrow staircase, pushing his gloved hands deep into the pockets of his coat. Using another key, Chip opened the outside door. A flurry of thick snow swept around them as they stepped out onto the roof.

Noah's boots sunk into the snow, but knowing he didn't have to trek anywhere comforted him. After Chip closed the door, they walked across the roof to the edge of the building. The view took Noah's breath away. He squinted through the snow at the lights of the city.

"Wow," Noah whispered. "This is what you call a view."

"I've never seen London so quiet," said Chip, leaning against the low wall and pulling his hipflask out of his back pocket. "I come up here sometimes when everything gets to be too much. Really puts things in perspective."

Noah had a similar feeling whenever he looked out of his seventh floor flat window. Seeing the rest of the world getting on with their lives always made his problems seem so small.

Noah accepted Chip's hipflask, and he took a deep swig of the warming whiskey. The hot amber flowed through his veins, warding off the cold. The sound of an engine pierced through the silence, and he looked down at a lone gritting truck crawling along like a snail, dispensing salt on the roads. It's spinning orange light lit up the dark streets, reflecting off the pure whiteness of the snow.

Even though he knew the city would be empty tomorrow, it reminded him of how busy the streets of London usually were, and how quickly life would resume when the holiday was over and the snow had melted.

"Do you regret what we did last night?" asked Noah, almost surprised by his own question.

Chip accepted back the hipflask with a frown deep in his brow. He took a deep sip, pulled his pink hat further down his face, and turned to Noah.

"Why would I regret it?" Chip mumbled, shaking his head, seeming genuinely surprised by Noah's question.

"You left pretty quickly this morning."

"Because I didn't want to make things awkward, Noah," he sighed, turning to look down at the back of the gritting truck as it crawled sluggishly around the corner. "I'm your boss. I overstepped a line."

Noah hadn't looked at it like that. He almost wanted to tell Chip about the crush he had had on him for the past two years, but he bit his tongue.

"I won't tell anyone," said Noah. "If that's what you're worried about. I told Amy, but I've already sworn her to secrecy."

"That's not what I'm worried about," he said calmly. "Sasha has probably told everybody she knows the truth. I'll be very surprised if everybody doesn't know in the new year."

"What are you worried about?"

Chip took more of the whiskey and wiped his mouth with the back of his purple glove. He offered Noah another drink, but he shook his head. As Chip slowly pushed the hipflask back into his tight, jean's pocket, he turned away from the view and leaned against the edge of the building, facing the opposite direction. Chip crossed his arms tightly across his wrapped up chest, his muscles threatening to burst through the tight-fitting clothes to expose his skin to the elements.

"I was emotional last night," started Chip. "Alcohol and guilt don't mix."

"Because of the divorce?"

"Partly," he said, smiling sadly. "I can't blame Sasha for acting like this. We separated six months ago, but we decided to keep it a secret. Neither of us wanted to admit to the world our marriage had failed so quickly. It was all a whirlwind, but the minute we settled into our married life, I knew I couldn't live a lie again. I didn't tell her why we needed to separate, so we kept living under the same roof. I was surprised by how well she accepted it. She must have known we weren't right for each other. I thought we could divorce peacefully and I wouldn't have to have my dirty laundry dragged through public again. I wish I could say I was the one who told her the truth about me, but I wasn't. I was a coward."

"How did she find out?"

"Internet search history," he said with a heavy eye. "How else? Two weeks ago, she went back through looking for some shoes she wanted to order and I hadn't been clever enough to be more careful about what I searched for on my laptop. That's when she started telling people we were divorcing and it all blew up. She stopped being calm about it and she lost her mind. I don't blame her. Who wouldn't?"

"It surprised me," admitted Noah. "You always seemed so –"

"Masculine?" chuckled Chip, darting his eyes up to the pink hat on his head. "It was a rod to beat me with. People always just assumed I was straight, and with my father being so – y'know – it became harder and harder to be honest, so I just went along with it. I thought marrying and having kids would be easy if I found the right girl, so I just kept marrying women who I met and liked. You'd think in this day and age, with it being so easy and accepted to be yourself, I would have just done the right thing. It wasn't that easy. When people have a certain idea of who they think you are, it's so hard to suddenly say 'hey guys, everything you thought you knew about me is actually wrong'."

"You told me."

"That was easy," said Chip, as though that should have been obvious. "I can talk to you."

"And not because I'm gay?"

"No," said Chip, his brows arching. "Because you're a nice guy. I've always liked you, Noah, which is why I was ashamed of what I did last night. You were drunk, I was drunk. It shouldn't have happened, but I don't regret that it did. It was –"

Chip's voice suddenly trailed off and he looked down at the ground, his face screwing up tightly. He shuffled his foot in the snow, carving out a circle.

"I wanted it to happen," said Noah. "You didn't take advantage of me. I felt like I was taking advantage of you."

"Really?" Chip said with a laugh, seeming surprised.

Noah knew it would be a perfect time to confess his crush, but he didn't want to come across as creepy. Achieving his ultimate sexual fantasy seemed like something he was just ticking off some sordid list, but it wasn't like that. He had always been sexually attracted to Chip, but he was finding that he was growing attracted to him in other ways as well.

"Even if I was sober as a judge, I wouldn't have stopped it."

"You're just saying that," said Chip, gritting his jaw. "I should have known better."

"I'm being serious," said Noah, gripping Chip's

arm and looking him deep in the eye. "You're just a good guy who always thinks they have to do the right thing, but what happened last night, that wasn't wrong. It was too good to be wrong."

"Just good?" said Chip, his frown turning up into a smile.

"It was the best sex I've ever had in my life," said Noah, a little too honestly.

"Now I *know* you're just trying to make me feel better."

Noah let go of Chip's arms and grabbed the snow-covered lapels of his trench coat. He pulled Chip in and joined their lips. As their mouths opened to each other, Noah closed his eyes. Fire coursed through his veins, deceiving his senses.

When he pulled away, Chip's eyes were still closed and his lips parted. When he finally opened them and closed his mouth, he smiled.

"I would never lie to make you feel better," said Noah.

"How does this hat look?"

"Awful."

They both laughed. Noah let go of his lapels and dusted them down, readying them for more snow.

"I'm glad you came here," said Chip, in a low, husky tone.

"Me too."

"Shall we go back inside?" said Chip, darting his

eyes over to the door. "I can't feel my balls and I'm starting to worry."

Noah stopped himself from making a joke about feeling his balls for him, instead just supressing a smirk and nodded. He followed Chip to the door, and back down the dark corridor.

Despite being frozen, his heart burned in his chest, forcing him to wonder if he had more than just a crush on Chip Harington.

CHAPTER *Ten*

Noah woke up on Christmas morning in the arms of a beautiful man, snuggling under a duvet on the floor of an office. He stared up at the twinkling fairy lights and as the cold morning sun pushed through the blinds, he pushed himself further into Chip's warm body.

Chip stirred from his sleep with a smile and pulled Noah tighter into his body. They were both naked but they hadn't had sex. Instead, they had spent the night cuddling, talking about their childhoods while watching the lights that were wrapped around the cardboard Christmas tree twinkle and change colour.

"Merry Christmas," Chip whispered, kissing Noah's forehead.

"Merry Christmas."

Five minutes later, they were drinking filtered coffee in the boardroom, completely naked, looking out of the window and watching the snow continue to fall. Noah sipped his coffee with a smile, wondering how things had changed so much since drinking coffee in his kitchen only yesterday morning.

Chip stood up and walked through the open kitchen door. Noah admired the view of his round arse as he bent down and grabbed something from the bottom shelf.

"How does smoked salmon and pâté sound for breakfast?" Chip called over his shoulder.

"Like something a director would eat."

"Good point."

"You know there's cereal in the staff room."

"And there's milk in here," said Chip, grabbing the carton of milk and turning around with a grin.

Noah hurried off to the cold staff room and grabbed a box of cornflakes. When he returned, Chip had set two bowls on the table, along with two spoons, and fresh coffee.

When they had finished their breakfast, Chip told Noah to stay where he was and ran back into his office. Noah finished the last of his coffee and walked over to the window. The snow didn't look like it had stopped falling all night, making the gritting truck's efforts useless.

Noah didn't hear Chip sneak back into the room, but he felt his soft hands slowly wrap around his waist, and Chip's body push up against his. His stomach turned when he felt Chip's cock push up against his arse cheeks. Soft, gentle lips caressed his neck as Noah turned his head. He gave in and closed his eyes.

"Merry Christmas," Chip whispered as he pushed a small, white envelope in Noah's hands.

"Oh," said Noah, turning around, his own cock already starting to harden. "What's this?"

"A present," Chip beamed, taking his seat back at the boardroom table. "It's what people do on Christmas morning, right? Turns out, the shops don't open today, so this was the best I could do."

Noah leaned against the cold glass, not caring that his bare backside was pushed up against the window. If anybody was brave enough to venture out into the blizzard on Christmas morning, the least of their worries was Noah's naked body. He turned the envelope over in his hands and his stomach fluttered when he saw his name in Chip's handwriting. A small, sloppily drawn heart joined the end of the 'h' in his name.

"Open it," urged Chip.

The envelope felt light, almost empty in his hands.

It's recently dampened seal opened with ease, and he pulled out a small, compliment slip, branded with the company's logo.

"'*I owe you a pay rise*'," Noah read aloud, his brow furrowing.

"I was thinking twenty percent, or something," Chip said proudly. "I'll have to draw up the paperwork in the new year, but it's as good as a done deal."

"This is too much."

"It's the least I can do."

"No, this is really *too* much," said Noah, putting the paper on the table and pushing it away. "I can't accept this."

Chip looked up at Noah like a hurt puppy, reaching across the table to pick up the slip. He looked down at it, before looking back up at Noah, his face somewhere between hurt and confused.

"Oh," said Chip, forcing a smile. "Why not?"

"I didn't earn it," said Noah, looking down at the envelope still in his hands. "I appreciate the gesture, I really do, but I can't take it."

"I thought everybody wanted a pay rise?" Chip scratched the side of his head, dropped the paper and leaned back in his chair. "I thought you'd appreciate it."

"That's the point," said Noah. "Everybody wants a pay rise. London is expensive and it's not getting any cheaper. I don't want a pay rise because I slept with the boss. It's not right."

Noah almost felt guilty. It saddened him how hurt Chip looked by his refusal of the gift. He knew it had been given with the purest intentions, and the money wouldn't hurt things, but he wouldn't be able to live with himself next time he heard Amy say she was struggling to pay her electricity bill.

"You really are a selfless person," said Chip, reaching out and screwing up the paper. "I didn't even think that through. You're right. Just so you know, I do notice the hard work you put in. You're always the first and last here most days. You do deserve a pay rise."

"So give me one when you give everyone else one," said Noah, walking back around the table and sitting down next to Chip. "And make it the normal three percent."

"Three percent?" Chip arched a brow.

"Make it four if you're feeling extra generous," said Noah with a reassuring smile.

Chip looked down at the screwed up paper in his hands before tossing it into the paper wastebasket.

"Deal," he said. "I feel bad I haven't given you anything now."

"Just being here is enough," said Noah, looking around the boardroom. "I thought I was spending Christmas alone, and now I'm not."

"You're stuck with me, is what you mean?" Chip

smirked.

"Something like that."

"Shall we have some fun?" Chip asked, his voice suddenly light. "It is Christmas, after all."

"What did you have in mind?"

"This isn't what I had in mind," said Noah, gripping hold of the office chair handles.

"It will be fun!" exclaimed Chip.

"Are you sure you want to do this?"

"Aren't you?"

"Not now that I'm staring it in the face," mumbled Noah, tightening his grip on the handles even more, and doing the same with his toes.

"I've always wanted to do this."

"You have?"

"Hold on tight," Chip whispered in his ear. "Are you ready?"

"No!"

"Tough!" cried Chip. "Go!"

Holding onto the back of the chair, Chip pulled Noah back and started to run, before pushing with all his strength. Crying out and clenching his eyes tightly shut, Noah sped along the polished marble reception floor. In his mind, he could clearly see himself not slowing down, crashing through the doors and finally catapulting through them and into the snow.

Noah opened his eyes just in time to see himself

crash through a dozen snow and blood splattered cardboard Christmas trees. His chair spun and ground to a halt.

"Seven!" cried Chip, doing a decent impression of Len Goodman from *Strictly Come Dancing*.

Feeling dizzy, Noah stumbled out of the chair and looked down at the cardboard trees. When Chip had told him he'd always wanted to play office bowling, this wasn't what he had expected.

"Your turn!" cried Noah as he picked up the cardboard trees. "No excuses!"

"I was born ready," Chip cried back, his voice echoing around the vast, empty office, as he bounced naked on the spot, like a boxer waiting to enter the ring.

When Noah had picked up the last Christmas tree, he dragged the chair back to Chip, who was waiting for him with open arms. After he hugged and kissed Noah on the forehead, he sat in the chair, holding onto the handles tightly.

"It's a lot scarier from this angle," Chip mumbled. "Maybe you should move me closer."

"*No excuses!*" Noah hollered as he dragged the chair back.

Using every ounce of strength he had, he ran forward with the chair. He let go and Chip whizzed across the polished floor, seeming to go faster than Noah had. He watched, open mouthed, as Chip burst through the Christmas trees with open arms, knocking every single tree down. When his chair tipped, he fell off to be buried by a stack of cardboard trees, Noah let out a small yelp and ran towards the glass doors of the building.

"Chip?" he cried, as he waded through the mass of cardboard. "Are you okay?"

Chip appeared through the cardboard. If it hadn't been for the laughter, Noah would have thought he was wincing in pain. Chip grabbed Noah's hand and pulled him down on top of him. Their naked bodies pressed up against each other as they both laughed.

"I knew those trees would come in handy," Chip whispered when the laughter died down.

"I'm just glad the security cameras aren't turned on."

"I turned them back on," said Chip, the laughter stopping completely. "I wanted to capture the glorious moment I whooped your arse at bowling."

Noah's heart skipped a beat and he instantly looked up to the camera he knew was positioned right over the entrance.

"You're joking, right?"

Chip joined him in looking up at the camera, his expression serious and stern, before finally cracking up laughing again.

"Of course I'm joking," he wheezed, wiping a tear from the corner of his eye. "Imagine if somebody saw this."

Noah turned his head to the glass doors and windows, which were buried under twelve inches of snow. Anybody could walk past, and likely call the police when they saw them naked in a pile of blood tainted Christmas trees.

"Let them watch," said Chip, wrapping his hands around Noah and resting them on his backside. "There's nothing wrong with two men enjoying their Christmas morning."

Noah took advantage of the opportunity and leaned in to kiss Chip. He felt both of their cocks twitch, so he pulled away before he did something he would probably regret in full view of the street, no matter how empty it seemed to be.

"What else did you have on your list of '*things the boss can't do in the office but has always wanted to*'?" Noah asked Chip as he helped him up to his feet.

Chip smirked and leaned in, whispering something in Noah's ear.

"Now I know *this* one is a joke," said Noah.

Chip winked, bit his lip and shook his head. He intertwined his fingers around Noah's and dragged him back to the staircase.

CHAPTER
Eleven

ine looks life Africa," said Noah, tilting his head, squinting at the black and white picture.

"Mine looks like an alien."

"Let me see."

They exchanged photocopier pictures of their arses and they both tilted their heads at the same time.

"Is it upside down?" mumbled Chip.

"I don't know," Noah mumbled back.

"Let's look at the other ones."

Chip picked up the penis photocopy pictures out of the tray, and his head recoiled. He handed one to Noah, but Noah wasn't sure if he was even looking at a penis, never mind his own.

"You could blow these up, stretch them over canvases and put them on the walls," said Chip as they swapped papers again. "This is the sort of crap that passes as art these days."

"If you do that, expect my resignation on your desk."

"It might be worth it just to see your reaction," said Chip, his tone serious.

"You've been my boss for so long, I can never tell if you're joking," Noah muttered, squinting his eyes.

"Fun, isn't it?" Chip winked. "Well, I guess I can tick '*photocopy my genitals*' off that list."

Chip gathered the four pieces of paper and shuffled them together.

"And now to shred them," said Noah. "That was the deal."

"Oh, no." Chip turned around and scurried toward the office. "I'm keeping these ones."

"It was a deal!" cried Noah, chasing after Chip. "You promised!"

"I crossed my fingers and I actually said '*pomise*', if you were listening properly," he chuckled like a schoolchild as he dashed between the cubicles and slipped back into his office. "How do you think I manage to keep a publishing company afloat in such hard times? I'm a shrewd businessman, Mr. Anderson."

Chip stuffed the papers into a filing cabinet, locked the door and held the keys out over his shoulder. Noah struggled to catch his breath after his sprint through the office. With the keys outstretched, Chip backed away towards the window.

"Give me the keys!" Noah panted, leaning on his knees. "I'll burn the things myself!"

Chip froze on the spot for a moment, a wicked smirk taking over his mouth and brows. He reached out his hand, making Noah think he was about to hand the keys over. Instead, he turned, unclasped the window and tossed them out into the snow.

"No!" Noah yelled. "Why would you do that?"

"Because I have a spare set in here somewhere," said Chip casually. "And you'll never figure out where. They're very discreetly hidden."

Chip closed the window and turned to face Noah. Noah tried to be angry, but as his eyes drank in the beautiful naked specimen of a man standing in front of him, it was impossible to feel any ill feelings for more than a split second.

"Promise me you won't show anybody those things, ever," said Noah, holding out an outstretched finger. "I don't want to be known as the '*photocopier dick*' guy!"

"I pomise."

"Did you just say '*pomise*' again?"

"Maybe," chuckled Chip. "I *promise*."

"Show me your fingers!"

Chip walked across the office, wrapped his hands around Noah's face and kissed him so deeply and passionately, Noah forget what they had been talking about.

"I promise," said Chip, his forehead leaning against Noah's. "Happy now?"

"Maybe," he whispered, dazed from the kiss. "What's next on your list?"

Chip let go of Noah and backed away. He sat on the edge of his desk and stared up at the ceiling, as though thinking hard about it. After nearly a minute of silent thinking, he shrugged and tossed out his hands.

"That's it," said Chip.

"That's it?"

"It was a pretty short list," he said. "Maybe there is one more thing, actually."

Chip's phone started to ring and vibrate, interrupting their conversation. Chip grabbed the phone, looked at the screen and quickly hurried out of the office.

"Bro," Chip's voice floated through. "Merry Christmas. How's the family?"

Chip's voice steadily trailed off as he walked further and further away from the office. Noah pulled on some underwear and sat behind Chip's desk. He looked through the half-open blinds at the sea of cubicles, wondering if Chip ever looked out and noticed Noah. Leaning back in the comfortable chair, he ran his fingers along the desk's glass edge, wondering what it was like to have an entire publishing house at his command. He didn't think he'd like the responsibility.

The top drawer was half open, and his own name jumped out at him. He checked to see if Chip was still on the other side of the building before carefully opening the drawer and pulling out the file.

He immediately recognised the revised contract he had stayed behind on the last day of work to finish. There was a small, yellow sticky note attached to the front, with a small hand written note from Chip, which read: '*Great work, as always, Noah*'. Running his fingers over the ink, he smiled. If he hadn't stayed behind to get the work finished, he wouldn't have spoken to Chip, and Chip most likely wouldn't have shown his face at the Christmas party. Even if he had, he wouldn't have found a reason to talk to Noah.

The thought of spending Christmas alone in his flat hadn't affected him two days ago, but now that he was spending it with Chip, he didn't want to imagine that it could have been any different.

He opened the drawer further so he could put the file back, but a thick manuscript commanded his attention. The sight of a manuscript in Harington Publishing House wasn't an unusual one, even if Chip Harington didn't personally deal with every book passing through the company. It was the name on the front of the manuscript that called to him.

Abandoning the contract, he wrapped his fingers around the manuscript and pulled it out of the drawer. It wasn't one of their internal copies, and the lack of a cover letter had Noah assuming it was an unsolicited manuscript, which was against company policy.

"*C. P. Harris*," Noah read the author's name aloud.

Noah immediately thought back to the time he discovered Chip's middle name was Percy, after having a private letter from his lawyer accidentally delivered to his cubicle. Amy had teased him for weeks, saying that when Noah and Chip finally married, they should call their first child Percy.

He wondered if it was a coincidence that the unsolicited manuscript in Chip's desk held his three initials. Even if '*Harris*' wasn't quite '*Harington*', it was close enough. He turned his attention to the title, '*Journey of the Mind*', which meant nothing to him.

Just as he was turning the first page to peek inside, a throat clearing made him jump away from it, as though it were about to explode.

"My brother and his family are spending Christmas in France," said Chip, as he spun his phone around between his fingers. "I see you've met my alter ego."

Noah looked from the manuscript to Chip, knowing there was no way he could excuse digging around in Chip's desk. Chip opened a plastic bag, pulled out some black underwear, and climbed into them.

"I didn't mean to pry," mumbled Noah, a sweat breaking out on his brow. "I was just -"

"It's okay," said Chip, sitting on the chair on the other side of the desk and picking up the manuscript. "It's not like anybody is ever going to read it."

Chip flicked through the papers before dumping the heavy volume on the desk. He avoided looking at it directly, as though he was embarrassed by its mere existence.

"So you wrote this?" Noah asked.

"Finished the thing last year," he sighed, looking past Noah to the window. "Waste of six years' work."

"Why is it a waste?" Noah asked, puzzled.

"Because it's never going to be published."

"You've lost me."

Chip half smiled and leaned across the desk to run his finger along the curling edge of the front page.

"What was your dream when you were a little boy, Noah?" Chip asked him, his dark eyes darting up to claim Noah's attention.

"I wanted to be Sherlock Holmes," he said confidently, not even needing to think about it. "Granddad was a huge Arthur Conan Doyle fan, so my bedtime stories were always filled with murder and mystery. It sort of influenced my decision to study law, but I didn't have the brains to go all the way with that."

"Doesn't that upset you?"

Noah thought about it for a moment, but he shook his head.

"I learned to let go of that dream a long time ago. I'm happy working here. Writing contracts and tying up the loopholes is satisfying."

"I'm glad you enjoy your work," Chip smiled, the corners of his eyes creasing.

"What was your dream?" Noah asked.

Chip glanced down to the manuscript and sighed, a sad smile tainting his lips.

"You're looking at it." Chip tapped the manuscript before pushing it away from him. "All one hundred and fifty thousand words of it. Maybe I should have given up my boyhood dream too."

Noah frowned, not quite following Chip's train of thought.

"But you finished the book," said Noah, picking it up and flicking through the pages. "I'd say you achieved your dream, wouldn't you?"

"We know better than anyone that writing it is just half the job," he smirked dryly. "How many of the first-time author manuscripts that pass through here do you think we publish?"

Noah thought about it for a second, before remembering Amy, who coordinated with the agents of first-time authors, had told him the figure in passing.

"About ten percent."

"It's more like seven," he said, shrugging softly. "The other ninety-three percent float from publisher to publisher, hoping to get picked up. You can't blame the system. Half of the new books published will fail in the market, and that's without factoring in the growing online market. It's a tough world out there."

"I still don't understand," said Noah with a nervous laugh. "You run this place. If anybody can get a book published, it's you."

Chip nodded his agreement, but he didn't look happy about that fact. He stood up, walked around the desk and opened a drawer near the bottom. He pulled out a stack of around twenty letters and dropped them in front of Noah.

"Rejection letters," he said. "Including one from this very publishing company."

"You rejected your own book?" Noah flicked through the letters until he spotted Harington Publishing House's logo. "That makes no sense."

"Remember when you turned down my promotion because you felt you hadn't earned it?" asked Chip.

A light bulb suddenly ignited in Noah's mind and he suddenly understood.

"You submitted anonymously," said Noah. "You wanted to be published on the merit of your work, not your name."

"My dad always used to say the money was in publishing, not writing. He laughed at me when I told him I wanted to be a writer, not a publisher. He died when I was eighteen, and I'd already been working here learning the ropes for two years, so I was sworn into the top and I became the new Mr. Harington."

All of that was far before Noah's time at the company, but he had heard whisperings about Mr. Harington Senior being a cantankerous old man, who had been stuck in his ways and close to driving the company into the ground.

"You should know better than anyone that rejection letters are just part of the game we're in," said Noah, brushing the letters to the side. "Every great author has the exact same story of being rejected over and over before finally finding somebody who wanted to publish them. Plus, there's other ways of doing it these days."

"I know," said Chip, nodding. "I know. I guess part of the dream was to prove my dad wrong, that I could do this and be good at it. Turns out, years running one of London's biggest publisher's has taught me nothing about writing a great book."

"I'm sure it's great," said Noah, resting his hand on the top of the manuscript.

Before Noah could ask any more questions, Chip scooped up the manuscript along with the letters, and he dropped them into the waste paper basket.

"Enough about that," he exclaimed. "Are you hungry? I think it's time for Christmas dinner."

CHAPTER *Twelve*

The Christmas cracker exploded, its goodies landing in Noah's lap. He picked up the orange Christmas hat and placed it on his matching hair.

"I got a whistle," said Noah, giving the plastic toy a quick blow. "And a crap joke. Who hides in the bakery at Christmas?"

Chip grinned across the table and shrugged, "Tell me."

"Mince spies."

"Ouch," chuckled Chip. "No wonder there was so much food left over from the Christmas party. The directors were so put off by the jokes, they had no room for food."

"I don't know why." Noah took a bite out of the succulent turkey leg. "This has all been delicious."

Chip jumped up and walked to the edge of the table where all of the food had been displayed, after a quick blast in the microwave. Noah leaned back in his chair, a food belly already starting to develop.

"Speaking of mince spies," said Chip, as he walked over wearing his tuxedo apron. "Mince pie, sir?"

"I couldn't possibly," said Noah, reaching out for the tray. "But seeing as it's Christmas."

Chip bowed and walked back over to his seat, giving Noah a view of his beautiful, exposed backside through the apron. Christmas had always been a quiet affair for Noah. In his early years, it always consisted of a simple dinner with his Granddad, and in more recent years, in the nursing home. Even though it was just him and Chip, it felt perfect. He was touched by how much effort Chip had gone to, to inject Christmas spirit into everything. The flat-screen TV on the wall displayed a crackling fireplace, the radio was softly playing Christmas music, the heating was turned up so much Noah felt like he was in a tropical climate, and Chip had somehow managed to rustle up an almost perfect Christmas dinner using leftovers and a microwave. If Chip had been responsible for the snow too, he would have pulled out the perfect Christmas.

"I don't usually like sprouts," exclaimed Chip as he picked one up from the leftovers on his plate, "but these are rather delicious."

"I was always that weird kid who liked them." Noah jabbed his fork into one of the remaining gravy soaked sprouts and crammed it into his mouth.

"If I eat anymore, I'm going to pop," sighed Chip as he put another sprout in between his teeth.

"I thought that was the whole point of Christmas?"

"I suppose it is," admitted Chip. "More champagne, sir?"

"Why not?"

"Well, there are many reasons why not," said Chip as he picked up the bottle and leaned across the table, a lazy grin on his face. "But let's look at the reasons why we should."

"Champagne is delicious?"

"Quite, sir," said Chip, with a wink. "I hope I have served you well tonight."

"You've done quite well," Noah joked. "Although I have to say, your uniform is quite lax."

"Lax, sir?" Chip looked down at his apron. "What's wrong with a tuxedo printed on an apron?"

"It's hardly proper, is it, Mr. Harington?"

"Well, sir, I do apologise," sighed Chip as he stood up. "Would you prefer if I took it off?"

Noah scratched his chin as he pretended to think

about it for a moment.

"I think I would, Mr. Harington."

"As you wish, sir," Chip sighed, almost seeming aggrieved as he untied the apron from around his waist. "It's a good job we have this fire, sir, or else I might freeze."

Chip pulled the apron over his head, so that he was once again in just his underwear, just like Noah. He walked over to the video of the fire crackling on the TV, rubbing his hands together.

"Won't you join me by the fire, sir?" asked Chip over his shoulder with a grin. "It's mighty cold in here."

Noah took the napkin from his knee, screwed it up, and dumped it on the plate. He pushed out his chair and walked over to the TV, joining Chip. For a moment, he watched Chip pretend to warm his hands against the screen, before rubbing his own hands together and joining in.

"You'll catch your death wandering around in just your underwear," remarked Chip, "but the hat is quite fetching, sir."

"Thank you, Mr. Harington," said Noah, suppressing a smirk. "I must say, you look better without the hat. In fact, I'd go as far as to say clothes just don't do you justice."

Chip dropped his hands and turned to face Noah. He hooked his thumbs in the elastic of his underwear, giving Noah a tantalising view of the dark hairs surrounding his manhood and trailing up to his navel. Despite having spent all day naked together, this flash made Noah's stomach jump, as well as his cock.

"I could always take them off?" asked Chip. "If that's what sir really likes."

Noah gulped as he felt his cock harden in his underwear. It wasn't long before Chip noticed and looked down, a playful smirk consuming his face.

"Is that a Christmas cracker, sir?" whispered Chip.

"I don't know."

"You're supposed to say '*give it a pull, and we'll see*'."

They both laughed for a moment before Chip reached out and cupped Noah's face in his hands. Noah's heart pounded so hard in his chest, he was sure he could feel the heat of the fake burning logs on his shoulders. Closing his eyes, Noah wondered how things had turned out so perfectly. He made a silent prayer, wishing Christmas would last forever.

He felt Chip's hot breath on his face as he started to lean in to kiss him. Noah opened his eyes, wanting to remember the moment. He allowed himself to get distracted by something peculiar on the other side.

Turning his head, he squinted through the foggy glass, Chip's kiss catching him on the cheek.

"The snow's stopped," said Noah, his stomach turning unsurely. "I can see the sky."

Chip frowned and opened his eyes. He turned around and they walked over to the window. Chip wiped the condensation off of the glass, revealing a clear, blue and pink sky clinging onto the last of the day's light.

"What now?" asked Noah, expecting this to mean an end to being locked in the building.

"Well, I did have something in mind," said Chip, glancing down at the bulge in Noah's underwear. "But that can wait until later. I've got a better idea."

Chip looped his fingers around Noah's and pulled him back towards the office. Noah smiled, allowing himself to imagine the perfection spanning beyond Christmas. He knew it was a long stretch, but it was a glimmer of hope to hold onto.

Noah hesitated at the front door of the tower block, staring down at the divide between the white marble tiles and the snow. He looked back to the staircase, the cardboard Christmas trees still cluttering the reception. Exhaling deeply, he pulled on his gloves and stepped outside.

Looking up at the sky, he let the cold nip refreshingly at his skin. After spending so long in the sweltering office, it was nice to feel the crisp, December air on his skin. It almost made him forget it had only been yesterday that he had been trekking through it and almost froze to death.

"Heads up!" cried Chip.

A snowball jabbed Noah's arms. He spun around to see Chip stumbling backwards, a childlike grin on his face as he attempted to roll another snowball.

"Are you declaring war?" cried Noah, his voice echoing off the empty buildings.

"So what if I am?"

Noah doubled over and scooped up a ball of snow. Chip froze to the spot as Noah patted it between his hands. Trying his best not to embarrass himself, Noah tossed the snowball and it proudly landed in the middle of Chip's chest.

"It's on!" declared Chip.

Instead of bending over to pick up more snow, Chip turned on his heels and started sprinting along the snow covered road. He turned the corner and vanished from sight, leaving Noah standing alone in the middle of the deserted city streets. Glancing over his shoulder, it was easy to feel like he was the only person on the planet at that moment in time. He had spent so much of his life alone, that idea didn't scare him as much as it would other people, but he had to admit he liked knowing Chip was just around the corner.

Noah scooped up more snow and set off following Chip's deep footprints in the untouched snow. The gritting truck from the night before had poured its salt in vain because the snow had fallen as quickly as it had melted.

Turning the corner, Noah glanced in either direction, looking down the empty streets. He stared up at the skyscrapers around him, noticing how beautiful it looked to watch the reflection of the heavy clouds against the many windows. Night was creeping in, but the street lamps hadn't flickered to life yet.

Crawling along and patting his snowball, Noah cast his eyes into the dark doorways, expecting to see Chip huddled in one, ready to pounce. After a couple of minutes of searching, he was beginning to wonder if he really was alone in London.

Out of the blue, he heard the crunch of heavy boots on the snow, and without a second thought, he spun and tossed his snowball. He was so proud when it hit his target square in the face, but that feeling quickly melted away when he noticed it wasn't Chip.

"What the fuck do you think you're playing at!" boomed the stranger in a deep, East End voice. "Do you think you're a joker, lad?"

Noah mumbled over his words, backing away as the wrapped up man stepped off the invisible side of the pavement and onto the road towards him.

"I'm s-s-sorry," he stuttered, trying and failing to inject some humour into his voice. "I thought you were somebody else."

Noah would have seen the funny side of the mistaken identity, but he could practically see the smoke about to spit out of the man's ears. His wide, potato-like face had turned the colour of a beetroot, and his pale eyes were so wide, they looked like they might reflect the sky the same way the buildings did.

He could do nothing as the man's fingers closed around the front of his jacket. Running away had been the only thing he could think about, but fear had fused his boots with the snow. Instead of trying to do anything of use, he clenched his eyes and covered his face.

He waited for the blow, but it never came. Instead, the man suddenly let go, and there was a loud thump. Noah stumbled backwards, grateful for the lucky escape. He watched Chip wrestle the man to the ground, pinning him into the snow. Next to Chip, the man suddenly didn't look so big.

"You think it makes you big to pick on people smaller than you?" Chip cried, pushing the man further into the snow. "Huh? Do you?"

"He snowballed me!" the man cried, sudden nerves tainting his vocal chords. "He had it coming to him."

"It's bloody Christmas!" said Chip. "Get out of here."

The man scrambled to his feet, looking like he was going to try and take them both on at once. Instead, he spat into the snow, tossed his hands out and turned around. When he disappeared from view, Chip cupped

Noah's face in his hands, concern filling his hazel eyes.

"Did he hurt you?" Chip asked.

"I'm fine," Noah said with a smile, embarrassed at the mess he had caused. "It was my own fault. I thought he was you. I got him in the face."

"Good," Chip said with a wink. "The idiot deserved it."

Chip leaned in and kissed Noah gently on the forehead, melting his fear away in an instant. Noah was glad he wasn't the only person in the world after all, because being alone would never compare to the raging fire Chip ignited deep within him.

They walked back to the building, but instead of going inside, their snowball fight started for real. It took Noah more than a couple of attempts to properly hit Chip, but when his nerves eased, he got in a couple of good hits. When they called a cease-fire, they collapsed into the fluffy snow, laughing.

"I've never had anybody fight for me before," said Noah, making a snow angel in the untouched snow. "My Granddad always said I should learn to defend myself, but I never liked the idea of hitting somebody. I started Karate lessons then quit when we started practising what we'd learned on each other."

"Most of the time you just have to scare them enough," said Chip. "Making them think you're going to hit them is just as powerful."

"I could never come across as powerful as you,"

admitted Noah.

Chip stopped making his snow angel. He sat up and looked down on Noah, a deep frown forming in his brow under his pink hat.

"You have more power than you think," said Chip quietly. "You're a special person, Noah."

Chip's sudden sentiment made Noah instantly smile. His stomach knotted, so he forced himself to sit up. He knew his body felt cold, but Chip's presence was enough to warm him.

"You're pretty special yourself."

"Me?" scoffed Chip. "I'm not. Look at me. I'm thirty-two and soon to be divorced three times. I couldn't even come out of the closet without overthinking how everybody would react. To tell you the truth, up until yesterday I was considering trying to cover it up again. Only Sasha knew. I thought maybe I could talk her around, make her see sense to not tell people."

"Why would you do that?"

"Because it's easier," he sighed. "Easier than being honest."

"What made you change your mind?"

Chip smiled and looked down. He traced his finger around in a figure-of-eight in the snow.

"You did," said Chip finally. "You're so optimistic and full of hope. It's rubbed off on me."

Noah wondered if that was really true. As a child,

he could never imagine a life without his Granddad, but he had slipped away so slowly, Noah had somehow coped. He looked up to the sky, hoping his Granddad had been right about him being up there and looking over him.

"I chose not to be a victim of circumstance," said Noah.

"Victim," mumbled Chip. "I always thought I was a victim of my marriages and trying to make them work. The only people who were victims were the women I dragged into my mess. As of today, this very moment, no more hiding. Why do I need to hide?"

"People will care less than you think."

"It's not what they think that bothers me," he said. "It's what I think about myself. The thought of people knowing that I've been lying all this time scares me more than the thought of them knowing that I'm gay."

"It's not lying, it's just not showing the whole picture. We're all hiding something."

Chip smiled gratefully down on Noah. Noah could have stayed there all night, but the sound of the gritting truck's siren echoed down the empty street, soon followed by its orange flashing light. Chip helped Noah up off the road, and they headed back into the safety of the building.

As they walked up the stairs and back to their Christmas hideaway, Chip suddenly stopped in his tracks and turned around. He pulled off his hat and looked down at Noah from the step above.

"If everybody is hiding something, what are you hiding?" Chip asked.

Noah gulped, his throat suddenly turning dry. He thought about admitting his crush, knowing Chip would probably see the funny side now. The words were on the tip of his tongue, but he bit it. It wouldn't be so hard to tell him if it was just a crush, but it felt like so much more.

Amy had always told him he would probably hate Chip if he really got to know him, but now that he had, Noah was feeling the complete opposite emotion of hate.

CHAPTER
Thirteen

When their snow clothes were drying on the radiator in the hallway, they retreated back to the warmth of Chip's office and closed the door. Instead of turning on the fluorescent lights, Chip opted for the twinkling fairy lights as the last of the sun finally faded from the pastel sky.

Chip turned on a small radio, and Christmas music softly filtered through invisible speakers in the corners of the room. The lights danced along to Mariah Carey's '*All I Want For Christmas*', as though they had been programmed to do so. Ignoring the sofa or the chairs, Noah sat on the duvet in the middle of the floor wearing nothing more than his underwear. Hugging his legs to his body, he rested his head on his knees, watching Chip pop the seal on Noah's supermarket wine. Glancing over his shoulder, Chip smiled as he filled two of the company's branded mugs.

"Do you know how beautiful you look right now?" asked Chip.

"I was just thinking the same thing."

"I'm glad you agree how beautiful you are," quipped Chip as he handed Noah a mug.

"I was talking about *you*."

"Hush now," Chip said, taking a sip of his wine and sitting on the duvet next to Noah.

For a moment, they sat in silence, sipping their wine and listening to the Christmas music, content with the low glow of the lights, and the warmth from the gas heater.

A ringing and vibrating phone broke the silence. Noah recognised his own ringtone and sprung up. He dug through the pile of clothes on the floor and pulled out his phone for the first time since he had arrived at the office.

"It's Amy," he said apologetically.

"Take it."

Noah excused himself and hurried across the dark

office. His instincts took him straight to his cubicle, so he sat in his chair and answered the phone.

"Amy," he said. "How's it going?"

"Dude!" she cried down the phone, the buzz of her large family in the background. "I've been texting you all day. What's up?"

"My phone's been on silent," he lied.

"Wanted to forget it was Christmas?"

Noah glanced over his cubicle into Chip's office. "Something like that."

"I was beginning to wonder if you'd put your head in the oven or something."

"You know I have an electric oven," he chuckled. "I'm fine. How's Granny's?"

"Insufferable," she mumbled, and it sounded like she was walking into a quieter room and closing the door behind her. "My entire family is mental. My dad was drunk before dinner was served and he punched my uncle. Gran went ape shit, kicked them both out, and now I think they're both sulking in the pub."

"Jesus Christ, Amy."

"You're lucky you don't have any family," she sighed. "Is it too much to ask for one quiet Christmas?"

Noah paused, unsure of what to say. Amy groaned, clearly catching her own stupidity.

"I'm such an idiot," she moaned. "Sorry. I didn't mean it like that."

"I know what you meant," he said cheerfully, not wanting her to think she had upset him. "To tell you the truth, my Christmas hasn't been so bad."

"Dinner for one and crap Christmas movies?"

"Something like that," he said, smirking to himself as he fiddled with a pen on his desk. "Nothing too exciting."

"Thought anymore about boss man?"

"Not really," he lied.

"It's probably for the best," she sighed. "Steve has been ignoring my texts since the party. Maybe it's better we don't speak about our Christmas party mistakes. *Fuck off Brian! Can't I have a piss in peace?* My nephews are such little shits."

Noah laughed and glanced over his desk again. This time, Chip's shadow was standing in the door, the soft glow of the fairy lights illuminating his outline.

"I'm going to have to go," he said.

"Go? What could you possibly have to do right now that's more important than me?"

"The microwave just pinged," he lied again, already standing up. "Christmas pudding is ready."

"Hmmm," she groaned. "Well, I'll see you in a couple of days anyway. I need to go shopping for a New Year's Eve outfit. I think I've gained ten pounds in the last two days so I'll need something nice and floaty. You always know what suits me, and before you say it, you're not backing out of New Year's Eve like last year!"

"Yeah, sure," he called down the handset. "Bye, Amy."

Before she could say anything more, he hung up and set off through the dark towards the glowing shadow.

"How is she?" asked Chip, his arms crossed across his thick chest as he leaned against the doorframe.

"Loud, vulgar, offensive," he said. "So, the usual."

Chip laughed as he backed into the office. To Noah's surprise, Chip grabbed his hand and pulled him back down onto the soft duvet. Noah collapsed onto Chip's frame, their faces only inches apart.

"Look what I found," said Chip as he reached out behind him into the cardboard box the fairy lights had come in. "Mistletoe."

He held the plastic sprig of mistletoe over their heads. Noah glanced up at it, his stomach fluttering. He felt his underwear twitch as he looked back down into Chip's hazel eyes.

"You know you don't need an excuse to kiss me," he whispered.

"I know," said Chip.

Chip pulled Noah's face down into a soft kiss. Noah stared deep into Chip's eyes, and he stared back. Noah's breath fluttered as he felt a connection stronger than anything he had experienced before. Chip pulled away, cupping Noah's face in his hands. For a moment, he looked up and stared at Noah, as though he were taking in a beautiful piece of art in a gallery. Their lips joined again, this time with a passionate explosion. Their lips couldn't move fast enough, their hands couldn't explore each other frantically enough, and Noah's cock couldn't ache any more.

Chip rolled Noah over, so that Noah was lying on the duvet. For a moment, Chip loomed over him, his Adonis frame nothing more than a glowing shadow. Noah gulped, looking down at Chip's underwear to see his cock pushing firmly against the fabric.

Chip dived in, catching himself with his hands. He planted a soft kiss on Noah's lips, but the kisses left his lips and danced to the tender flesh on his neck. Noah writhed on the soft duvet as Chip sucked and nibbled on the skin. It would leave a mark, but it was so firmly positioned on the bridge between pain and pleasure, Noah couldn't, and wouldn't stop it.

Using his tongue like an artist delicately painting a canvas, Chip worked down Noah's body, following the contours of his toned stomach. Chip reached the elastic of his underwear and he paused. His beautiful, dark eyes stared seductively up at him, making Noah's stomach knot tightly. Aside from the sip of wine, he was completely sober. He could almost forget he had already had sex with the beautiful creature peeling back his underwear.

Chip's hot breath hit the tip of Noah's cock. He peered up into Noah's eyes, a playful smirk tickling his features. When Chip's tongue made contact, Noah forgot how to breathe for a moment. He inhaled deeply and looked up at the fairy lights, feeling the warmth of Chip's mouth around him.

Noah brushed his fingers through his boss's hair as he bobbed up and down in a way that told him Chip had somehow done this before. It felt too amazing to be the touch of a first timer. Chip wasn't treating it like a race to finish, he was treating it like a dance. He knew when to slow and when to speed up, pushing Noah to the edge, and then dragging him back in the blink of an eye.

This dance continued for what felt like a lifetime, but Noah knew it couldn't have been more than a couple of minutes. When he couldn't take any more, he gripped Chip's short, dark hair in his fists.

Chip looked up to Noah, causing Noah to groan loudly.

"I'm close," he grunted, trying to contain his moaning. "So close."

Chip pulled away from Noah's cock and he kissed below Noah's navel, working his way back up. Noah leaned up, wrapping his hands around Chip's neck. Their lips touched again, and it was obvious they were both hungry for more.

They lowered down to the ground and they kissed

for what felt like an age, their bodies writhing up against each other. Chip's hand ran down Noah's body, gliding over his hipbone. Using his thick, firm fingers, Chip clutched Noah's cock, almost teasing him.

"Are you sure?" Chip asked him, looking down seriously into Noah's eyes.

For a moment, Noah thought Chip was trying to find a way to back out, even if his hand working his cock was saying a different thing. When Noah suddenly realised Chip was as nervous as Noah to do this sober, he was touched. It almost felt like their first time, all over again.

Noah didn't respond verbally; he didn't need to. Clenching his eyes tightly, he pushed his body even harder into Chip's, forcing the grip on his cock to tighten.

The kissing suddenly stopped and Chip rolled Noah over onto his side. Face pushing down against the duvet, Chip kissed his neck. Chip took the opportunity to peel down his own underwear, relieving the strain.

Noah heard the rip of foil and the snap of plastic. Arms wrapped around Noah, holding him in an embrace, he felt Chip's manhood line up between his cheeks. Closing his eyes, he let the urgent kisses on the back of his neck wash over him as he felt Chip's cock push through.

As Chip slowly pushed his length inside of him, Noah didn't resist. Gasping and clenching his eyes, he steadied his breathing, focussing on the sound of Chip's lips brushing against his neck.

When Noah felt Chip's full length inside him, he let out a loud moan, and pulled Chip's face in to kiss him. Chip's arms tightened around him, clinging onto him as he increased his rhythm.

Sweat formed between them as their bodies rocked in unison. Noah's mind floated above them, and he felt as though he was looking down on himself. He wanted to disbelieve it was happening, but every thrust and grunt from Chip felt as real as anything ever had, and he was glad of it.

Their tongues crashed together with little precision as Chip's hips bucked against Noah. When his grip on Noah suddenly loosened and his hand danced down Noah's stomach and clutched his cock once more, Noah knew what was happening.

Chip's hand matched his thrusts and it wasn't long before he was sending Noah dangerously close to the edge. When Chip whispered that he was close in his ear, Noah stopped trying to hold back and he unleashed.

His entire body tightened and his ears rang, blocking out the Christmas music on the radio. Chip's body suddenly turned rigid behind him after one last, deep thrust.

Noah's orgasm dragged out longer than he thought possible. Every pore in his body tingled with electricity. He wanted the feeling to last forever, but he knew all good things had to come to an end.

Chip pulled back and snapped off the condom. He collapsed onto the duvet, his stomach disappearing into his spine as he panted for breath. He opened his arm, signalling for Noah to cuddle up.

Noah fit into Chip's arm as though it had been designed that way. Chip wrapped his hand tightly around Noah's shoulder, pulled him in and kissed Noah on the top of the head. It was such a simple gesture, but Noah knew exactly what it meant. It felt like a promise of what they had done meant something.

Noah lay in the crook of Chip's arm as Christmas slipped away. He forced himself to stay awake long after Chip had started to softly snore. He let every detail of the day wash over him, running through everything with close precision. He didn't want to forget a single thought or feeling.

When he finally let his eyes flicker and he decided to give in to sleep, he drifted off knowing that nothing would ever make him forget his perfect Christmas day.

CHAPTER *Fourteen*

When Noah woke up in the morning, he felt the shift almost immediately. As he stared up at the fluorescent strip lights in the ceiling, he knew Christmas was over. Stretching out, he rolled over on the duvet but Chip wasn't there. Noah tried to ignore the parallels between now and the first time they had shared a bed.

He sat up and he caught Chip's voice. It was faint, as though he were on the other side of the office, but it sounded like he was arguing with somebody.

Noah jumped up and pulled on his t-shirt, which smelled stale after being worn two days in a row. He peeked through the blinds and saw Chip pacing between the cubicles, his fingers pinched between his brows as he spoke into his phone.

"You're being unreasonable!" Noah heard him say. "Can't we just talk and sort this out?"

Chip glanced over to Noah, making him snap the blinds shut and step back from the window. Scratching at the back of head, he turned around in the office, noticing that things were tidier than they had been when they had fallen asleep.

He crossed the office and his heart sank when he saw the pavements and the roads were almost clear of snow. Crowds of people marched up and down the streets, while buses and cars crawled along the road. It was almost as if none of it had happened.

Noah turned around when he heard the office door open. Chip hurried in, clutching his phone and rubbing his hands down his face.

"Morning," he said, almost distracted. "Sleep okay?"

"Yeah," said Noah, rubbing his neck. "The snow's melted."

Noah turned back to the window and stared down, almost resentfully, at the people below. Chip wrapped his hands around Noah's waist and he kissed his neck, but he didn't linger.

"There's some workmen coming to fix the lifts today," said Chip as he pulled away. "It was the only day they could fit us in over the holidays and I wanted it fixed before everybody got back."

"Oh," said Noah with a frown. "Okay."

Noah looked down at his clothes, and the bag of microwave pizzas and crisps. He couldn't tell if Chip was hinting that he needed to leave, but something felt off about the way he was acting.

"I should get home then," said Noah, almost hinting for Chip to stop him. "I need a shower."

"Good idea," said Chip, nodding as he stared through the window, his fingers drumming on the phone. "We can meet up later for lunch if you're not doing anything?"

Noah nodded his agreement. He forced a smile, feeling like it was a consolation prize for being kicked out. All of a sudden, the two days they had spent together felt like they were now trapped within a snow globe and Noah was desperately scratching at the glass to get back inside.

When he was dressed in the clothes he had arrived in, Chip walked him down to the front doors. Chip kissed him and gave him a hug, but Noah could feel how distracted his mind was. He almost asked who Chip had been talking to on the phone, but he decided against it.

"Meet me back here about two?" asked Chip as he

opened the door. "I'll take you somewhere nice."

"Two it is," said Noah, forcing a smile.

Within seconds, he was being swept away from Harington Publishing House in a sea of shoppers. He tried to look back to see if Chip was still at the door, but he couldn't see a thing. Instead of heading to the Tube station to take him home, he headed to the shops to buy a belated Christmas present.

Noah hadn't visited Springhill Nursing Home since his Granddad had died. He had promised himself that he was going to stop by on Christmas Eve, but Chip had derailed his plans.

Clutching the hamper he had just bought in a Christmas sale in an overpriced organic food shop, he left the cold London air and stepped into the warm reception of the nursing home. Balancing the hamper on a chair arm, he unravelled his scarf, took off his gloves, and banged the last of the snow off his boots.

"Noah?" a woman called from behind the reception desk. "Is that you? What are you doing here? I haven't seen you since –"

Noah recognised her as Nurse Smith, a kind lady in her late-fifties who had always been sweet to his Granddad. She was a short, slim lady, with greying brown hair pulled off her mousy face and pinned in a French roll at the back.

"I wanted to drop this off," said Noah, holding up

the hamper. "I should have done it sooner, but I wasn't expecting this weather."

Nurse Smith stood up, a warm smile filling her face as she wiped the smeared plastic wrapping.

"I don't think any of us expected this," she sighed. "The weather forecast never gets it right. Even with the heat on full, the residents are still freezing cold. We only have so many blankets and electric bar fires to go around. What's all of this in aid of, anyway?"

"I just wanted to thank you all," he said, almost nervous about even bothering to buy them something. "It's just some wine and some nice food bits. I know a lot of you worked over Christmas, so I wanted to show my appreciation."

Nurse Smith placed her hand on her heart as she peered through the plastic wrap. For a moment, Noah thought she was going to cry, but she held herself together. Pulling him across the counter, she planted a kiss on his frozen cheek.

"That's so kind of you," she said as she picked up the hamper and put it behind the counter. "I knew I always liked you for a reason! The girls will be over the moon when I show them this."

"We will?" asked another nurse who looked up from her clipboard as she walked through the reception area.

"Do you remember Sidney Anderson? His grandson has brought us a hamper to share out between the girls," said Nurse Smith proudly, holding it up like a prize on a game show. "Isn't that thoughtful?"

"That's so kind," said the nurse as she squeezed Noah's shoulder. "Your Granddad never stopped talking about how good a boy you were. Some of the living residents' families aren't that nice."

The reminder of his Granddad's death stung more than it should have. He was still feeling particularly sensitive after his strange morning with Chip. Noah tried to hide his pain behind a smile, but Nurse Smith seemed to spot it and she jerked her head, letting the other nurse know it was her time to move on.

"It really is very kind of you," she said softly, resting her hand on Noah's. "Sidney would be very proud."

"I didn't just come by to drop off the hamper," he said, glancing over to the residents' room, where he could see the elderly residents sitting under blankets in various chairs, all angled towards a TV – some of them had family members sitting next to them, some of them didn't. "I was just wondering if there was anyone who didn't get a visitor over Christmas? I thought I could sit with them for a while."

"You're such a good boy," she said as she hurried around the counter. "Come with me. I'll introduce you to Betty. She never had any children and the rest of her family popped their clogs years ago. You're going to make her entire Christmas."

Noah sat with Betty and talked with her for well over an hour. It only took her a couple of minutes to warm up to Noah before she started pouring the stories of her youth on him. When her lunch was brought out, he excused himself and headed back through to the reception.

Nurse Smith was reading a book and dunking a digestive biscuit in a milky cup of tea.

"Anything good?" he asked her.

"*The Cuckoo's Calling*," she exclaimed, showing him the cover. "Picked it up in a charity shop. Had no idea JK Rowling wrote it. She released under this man's name."

"Really?" he asked as he wrapped his scarf back around his neck.

Nurse Smith jumped up, cramming the biscuit into her mouth, seeming glad to tell Noah something he didn't know.

"Read about it in this magazine," she said, jabbing her finger on the top of the magazine pile on the counter. "Says she wanted to be a first-time author. Tons of publishing companies turned her down, because they didn't know it was her! Can you imagine? One of the bestselling authors in history can't get her book published. Just proves those big companies only go for famous names."

Noah flicked through the magazine and he landed

on the article she was talking about.

"Can I take this page?" he asked.

She ripped it out for him, folded it up, and handed it over, saying it was the least she could do. Noah thanked her, said his goodbyes and headed back out into the cold London streets.

He checked his phone, and he still had two hours to go until his meeting with Chip, but he suddenly felt like he couldn't keep away. Chip acting strange this morning didn't change the time they had spent together, and what they had shared with each other. With another author's success story in his pocket, he set off across London, determined to not let the perfect Christmas slip through his fingers so easily.

He pushed through the busy street and came up to Harington Publishing House. He was about to pull on the door, but he paused over the handle, looking wide-eyed into the dark reception area.

When he saw Chip and Sasha hugging in the dark, he dropped his hand and backed away. He pulled the magazine article out of his pocket, but his gloved fingers were shaking so much, he dropped it in the slushy, dirty snow.

Turning on his heels and dropping his head low, he headed straight for the Tube station at the end of the street, feeling like the snow globe had just been smashed and all of the Christmas joy within it had suddenly seeped away.

CHAPTER
Fifteen

Noah arrived at Amy's flat on New Year's Eve with a bottle of wine in his hands and a fake smile on his face. He couldn't be bothered with either, but Amy wouldn't let him back out, especially since she had spent an obscene amount of money on a new dress.

"Come in!" she beamed, pulling him into a tight hug. "I've missed your face! Everything's going tits up. My hair isn't cooperating, I can't level my eye liner, and I don't think I'm going to fit into that new dress."

"You'll be fine," he said, rather unenthusiastically.

Amy's flat was very similar to Noah's, in that it was small and messy, but she had put more effort into her decorating. Where everything was either from IKEA or second-hand in Noah's flat, everything in Amy's had been carefully selected from designer catalogues.

Amy hurried off to finish getting ready, leaving Noah to crack open the wine. He sat at her kitchen counter and poured himself a generous amount. He glanced to the clock, wondering how it could only still be nine in the evening. He took a deep sip of the wine, knowing it was going to be a long night.

"Can you see my food baby?" asked Amy, turning to the side and sticking out her stomach. "I tried to get something that would hide it, but I don't think it's working."

"You look fine. You're so skinny."

"Shut up."

With that, she vanished again, only to return ten minutes later with a round brush stuck in her thick hair. After Noah helped her untangle it, he decided to take his wine through to her bedroom. Dresses and makeup scattered her bed, so he cleared a small patch to perch on the edge.

"I hope I see Steve out tonight," she said as she applied her lipstick in the mirror. "I need at least one more go on that before we have to go back to work and pretend none of it happened."

"Maybe it's best that you don't," he mumbled, staring into his wine.

He tried not to let Chip wander into his mind, but it was difficult not to. He hadn't been able to think of anything else since seeing Chip hugging Sasha.

"Are you sure you're okay?" she asked him through the mirror. "You've got a face like a slapped arse, babe."

"I'm fine," he exhaled heavily, forcing a wide grin. "I'm just not sure I'm up for going out tonight."

"No backing out! Remember?"

"I know, I know. I'm here, aren't I?"

Amy abandoned her makeup and cleared a space next to Noah. She wrapped her arm around him and pulled him in.

"I get it," she whispered, resting her head on his. "Sometimes the dick is too good to forget."

Noah laughed. Amy always knew when to say the most inappropriate thing to cheer him up.

"I wish it were that simple."

"One-night stands never are."

Noah nodded and sipped his wine, letting Amy get back to finishing her makeup. She would never understand without knowing the full story, but he couldn't bring himself to tell her. As long as it existed in his memory, he could muster up that warm place just before reality came crashing back down.

"Right, I think I'm ready," said Amy, as she

wrestled on a shoe. "How do I look?"

"Beautiful," he said. "I'll call a taxi."

Noah had never understood why people tortured themselves with going into London on New Year's Eve. After over half an hour waiting at the bar, he finally took their drinks back to the table that Amy had managed to grab, which she was now sharing with a group of men.

"This is ridiculous," she cried over the thumping music as she sipped her cocktail. "It's never usually like this."

"It's like this *every* year, you're just usually drunk by the time we come out."

"I didn't want to bloat up on wine," she said, shrugging casually.

They continued this dance for the next couple of hours, finding new places, fighting their way to the bar, and then leaving in search of a better place. Noah was too distracted to even let the alcohol properly take effect.

In their fifth bar, and after waiting in line for the bathroom for twenty minutes, he locked himself in a stall and rested his face in his hands. He checked the time, glad that it was almost midnight. He knew Amy would want to stay out until the sunrise, but he hoped he could somehow slip away. He usually hated it when she let a random man attach himself to their group, but tonight, he was hoping for it.

He flushed the toilet and pushed his way through the crowded bathroom towards the sinks. He cupped water in his hands, before splashing it on his face. He looked in the mirror and watched as his pale skin turned bright red.

He was just about to leave the bathroom, when a familiar voice broke through the buzz of the club.

"Bro, this is crazy," the voice said. "Why did I let you talk me into this?"

Clinging on to the edge of the sink, Noah looked towards the men at the front of the line. At first, he thought it had been his imagination, but then Chip's face appeared from the crowd.

Without taking a second to think about it, Noah hurried out of the bathroom, wiping his wet hands on his jeans. With his head lowered, he pushed his way through the crowd, in search of Amy.

When he found her, she was sitting on a sofa with Steve. Their lips were locked and their hands were messily exploring each other's bodies over their clothes.

"Amy, I need to go," he cried over the music. "I can't stay here."

She reluctantly pulled herself away from the kissing, her red lipstick smudged, and her eyes half closed. He didn't doubt she had spent the last twenty minutes doing shots with whoever would buy them for her.

"Chill out, man," said Steve. "Noah, right? Amy was telling me about you. I have a friend. Technically straight, but he's known to dabble when he's had a few bevvies."

"What?" Noah mumbled, shaking his head. "Amy, I'm leaving. *He's* here."

"Who?" she asked, laughing as she glanced from Steve to Noah, clearly feeling conflicted.

"*Him*," he said through gritted teeth, not wanting to give away the name of their boss in front of Steve.

"*Oh*," Amy jumped up. "Where?"

"Bathroom," he said, tugging at his suddenly tight shirt. "I need to get outside. I need some air."

Amy looped her fingers through Noah's and dragged him through the crowd, screaming at anybody who dared get in her way. They pushed their way out of the bar and into the cold night, where it was lightly snowing once more.

"He's here," he said again. "Chip's here. I saw him."

"Are you sure?" Amy asked, stumbling as she pulled her cigarettes from her handbag. "Maybe it was just another hunk in a sharp suit."

They walked past the smoking area in front of the club and onto the pavement. The bouncer tried to usher them into the fenced-in smoking area, but Amy gave him the middle finger and cried that it was an emergency, and that their bar was shit anyway.

Amy offered Noah a cigarette but he declined.

"It's less than ten minutes until midnight," she said as she lit her cigarette. "Just stick around for ten more minutes and then we'll go."

"What about Steve?"

"Fuck Steve," she cried. "You're more important."

He was touched that Amy would sacrifice her own crush for him, but he wouldn't ask her to.

"Stay," he said. "I'm only going to go home and crawl into bed."

"You can't do that on New Year's," she pleaded, ash tumbling from her cigarette as she spoke. "I thought it was just a one-night stand? A bit of fun?"

Noah sighed and looked to the row of black cabs across the road. It would be so easy to excuse himself, jump into one, and see in the new year in the back of a taxi with a complete stranger. He knew he had to tell Amy the truth.

"I spent Christmas with Chip," he said reluctantly.

"What?" she spat out the word. "*How*?"

"It's a long story, but I was right about him sleeping in his office, so I went to see how he was. We got snowed in and we stayed there until Boxing Day."

"You mean you spent Christmas together, or you *spent* Christmas together?"

"The second one," he said.

"So it wasn't just a one-night stand?"

"I wish it were. It would have been easier."

Amy dropped her cigarette on the ground and stubbed it out under her shoe. She blew the smoke out of her lungs, her brows twisted in a frown.

"I'm not following," she said. "I thought that was your dream?"

"It was," he said, glancing over to the taxis. "It's hard to explain. The day after Christmas, he was acting weird, and then I left for a couple of hours and when I came back, I saw him hugging Sasha."

"The wife?" asked Amy. "But they hate each other."

Noah nodded and sighed, the thought of it sending a knife deep in his stomach.

"I thought so too," he said, wrapping his arms around his cold body as the snow steadily fell around them. "He told me it had been easier to lie all this time and that I'd made him see he could be open, but I guess that was all bullshit."

Amy's bottom lip curled down and she pulled Noah into a quick hug. He let her hug him for a couple of seconds, but he pulled away and stepped back into the road.

"I'm gonna go," he said.

"And leave me to see in the new year alone?"

"You've got Steve," he said, glancing over to the bar with a smile. "You won't be alone."

"But I want you here!" she cried, stepping carefully off the pavement and grabbing him by the wrist. "Just come back inside and you can go the second *Auld Lang Syne* finishes."

"I can't go back in there."

"Why not?" she pleaded, attempting to pull him back onto the pavement. "Don't let a man bring you down."

"It's not as simple as that."

Amy let go and hurried around him, blocking his way to the taxis.

"Sure it is," she cried, a manic smile on her drunken face. "You had a nice Christmas together and you had sex, but so what? It's a new year in," she paused to check her watch, "four minutes! It's a fresh start."

"I think I've fallen in love with him," he cried, a little louder than he intended. "That's why."

Amy's eyes widened and her mouth dropped open, but they didn't stay on Noah for long. They drifted over his shoulder and they widened even more. She nodded her head and coughed back towards the bar, making Noah turn.

Chip looked down on Noah, his eyes just as wide as Amy's, with his brows low over them.

"Noah," said Chip, stepping towards him. "I knew I saw you. I've been looking all over the bar for you."

"Chip," Noah mumbled, barely able to look him in the eye. "I was just going."

"I'll leave you two to it," whispered Amy,

squeezing Noah's shoulder carefully.

Amy hurried back into the club, leaving them alone on the pavement as the snow fell around them.

"Did you just say you'd fallen in love with me?" asked Chip, still frowning.

"I don't know what I said," he lied. "I'm drunk."

"You don't look drunk to me."

"Well, I am!" he cried.

Noah inhaled deeply, trying to calm down.

"I don't understand," whispered Chip, taking a step toward him. "When you didn't turn up for lunch, I just assumed –"

"I saw you and Sasha hugging," he interrupted. "I got the message."

"What? When?"

"I came back early to give you something, and I saw the two of you hugging in the reception at work. Don't try and deny it, I saw it with my own eyes."

"I'm not going to deny it," he said, still frowning. "I did hug her."

"You were acting weird when I woke up," said Noah. "I should have realised why."

Chip pinched between his brows and shook his head.

"I'm not following your train of thought, Noah," he said, laughing softly. "You were the one acting strange that morning. You packed your stuff and got out of there as quickly as you could."

"I thought that's what you wanted."

"Why would you think I wanted that?"

"The phone call," said Noah, suddenly feeling like he was clutching at straws.

"I was talking to Sasha," he said. "She said she wanted to see me. I thought she was going to try and squeeze more money out of me, or try to throw my sexuality back at me, so we argued. That's why I was distracted. When she turned up, we talked it out. I told her how I'd spent Christmas and how I thought I'd found somebody I really cared about, and we hugged it out. When you didn't turn up for the lunch date, I just assumed it wasn't the same for you. It hurt, but I wasn't going to force you. I've been in enough relationships to know when I'm pushing things in the wrong direction."

Noah absorbed all of what Chip was saying. It took him a moment to realise how wrong he was about everything.

"You care about me?" asked Noah, his voice barely there as he looked up into Chip's eyes.

"Incredibly," said Chip, resting his hand on Noah's cheek. "I've always liked you. It was just a silly thing, but I never thought anything would come of it. Spending Christmas with you was the happiest I think I've ever been."

"You liked me?" asked Noah, unable to hold back the laughter. "I've liked you since the moment I met you."

"Really?" Chip arched a brow and smirked. "You're just saying that."

"Ask Amy," he said. "I suddenly feel like an idiot now."

"Why?"

"Because I jumped to conclusions. I thought it was all too good to be true."

"You made me open up more than I ever have before," said Chip, his fingers caressing Noah's cheek. "You've worked for me for two years, but I feel like I grew closer to you while spending Christmas together than anybody I've ever known. I can't explain it, so when you didn't show up for lunch, I just assumed I'd misread things, as usual."

"I should have just talked to you about it," said Noah, pushing his face into Chip's hand. "I should have known you better than that."

"You've got plenty of time to get to know me even better," he said, grabbing Noah's face with both hands. "I want to be with you, Noah. I think I've fallen for you too."

At that moment, every bar around them began to chant down from ten. Noah closed his eyes and listened as the final seconds of the year ticked away. When it got down to 'three', he grabbed Chip and pulled him in. Their lips crashed together, and Noah's fears and reservations melted away. The sound of fireworks erupted around them as Chip wrapped his arms around Noah.

"You're supposed to wait until they say '*Happy New Year*'," whispered Chip through the kiss.

"I couldn't wait," he said. "I needed to kiss you one last time before the year ended."

Amy hurried out of the bar, dragging Steve behind her. Her lipstick was even more smudged than before. When she saw Noah and Chip holding each other, she jumped up and down and screamed.

"So does this mean you two are a couple now?" she cried, diving in to kiss Noah on the cheek.

Noah looked to Chip, who nodded.

"I think we are," said Chip, wrapping his fingers around Noah's.

Noah closed his eyes for a moment and he let the feeling of pure perfection wash around him. He wanted to disbelieve any of it was happening, but his heart burned too loudly for it all to be a dream. He squeezed Chip's hand and rested his head on Chip's shoulder.

"Are you still going home?" asked Amy.

Chip looked down to Noah, leaving the decision with him.

"I think we have something to celebrate," said Noah.

Amy grabbed Noah's hand and dragged him back towards the bar. Before they reached the door, Chip leaned into Noah's ear.

"By the way," Chip whispered softly. "I love you too."

EPILOGUE

One Year Later

Noah peered over the edge of his desk at Chip's office. Before he could get a good look at what his boss was doing, Amy handed him a glass of champagne and a plate of party food.

"Great idea to have the Christmas party at the office this year," mumbled Amy through a sausage roll. "This place really scrubs up. Have you seen the new art in the boardroom? It's bloody weird."

"I haven't been in there yet," he said, one eye still trained on Chip's office door. "What's he doing in there? He's been in there for ages."

"No idea," she said, running her fingers through his ginger hair. "Why don't you go and check up on lover boy?"

Noah's stomach fluttered, just like it did every time anybody reminded him that he had spent the last year in a relationship with the most perfect man on the planet.

"Some of the guys are playing some weird game of human bowling with a bunch of cardboard Christmas trees if you fancy it?"

"That's so last year," he said, winking at his best friend as he scooped up his champagne. "I'm going to go and check on him."

Noah left Amy in his cubicle and he walked across the office, squinting at the disco lights as he passed the DJ booth. He noticed Clark making out with their newest intern, Andy, and he smiled. Ever since those two had gone public with their relationship, they had been the latest office couple. Noah was glad all eyes were off him and Chip for once.

"Noah, can I have a word?" asked Beth, stepping in front of Noah just before he reached Chip's office door.

"I was just about to –"

"Do you know who my secret Santa was?" she whispered, pulling a pink vibrator out of her handbag. "This was left in my drawer, with a card saying '*Why don't you go fuck yourself. You look like you need it*."

Noah choked on his champagne and stared down the end of the vibrator like the barrel of a loaded gun. Amy hadn't told him who her secret Santa was, but he didn't doubt this was Amy's handiwork.

"No idea," he said, playing dumb. "There are worse presents."

"*A vibrator*?" she whispered, clicking the button so that the pink head twirled around. "What am I supposed to do with this?"

"Follow the instructions?"

With that, he stepped around Beth and knocked gently on Chip's office door. Even after a year of sharing a bed with the man, he couldn't bring himself to just walk in to his boss's office.

"Come in," he heard Chip call out.

Noah eased open the door and slipped into the office, glad to get away from the noise. Chip smiled at him, looking up from the letter he was reading under the glow of the lamp.

"I heard some of the guys have stolen your human bowling idea," said Noah, walking over to the desk and running his hand along Chip's shoulders. "What could be so important that you're missing your own office Christmas party?"

Chip grabbed Noah's hand and kissed the back of it, looking up into his eyes.

"My manuscript was accepted," said Chip quietly.

"The letter came through last week but I couldn't bring myself to open it."

"What?" Noah pulled the letter out of Chip's hands and quickly scanned the words. "This is amazing! It's with our rival, but who cares? I'm so proud of you."

"I told myself they would be the last publishers I submitted to, and they actually love the book," said Chip, taking back the letter with slightly shaking hands. "I can't believe I've finally done it."

"Dreams do come true."

Noah leaned in and kissed Chip on the top of the head.

"Come on," said Chip, stuffing the letter in the drawer and standing up. "Let's get some food and celebrate."

Chip took Noah's hand, led him out of his office and through to the busy boardroom. The large table was filled with food, much like it had been nearly a year ago when Noah had spent his Christmas with Chip. Christmas was only a couple of days away, and Noah couldn't be more excited to be spending it with Chip in their new apartment.

Noah picked up a plate and started to walk down the table, picking up sausage rolls and sandwiches, but the music suddenly stopped, making him turn around.

When he did, he saw the whole company standing behind Chip, with Amy right by his side. She was grinning from ear-to-ear, with her hands clasped together over her heart.

"What's going on?" asked Noah, glancing over his shoulder at the empty boardroom.

"Noah," said Chip, taking a step forward and reaching out for Noah. "This past year, I realised how happy I could be. You've shown me what it's like to love, and be loved, with a full, true heart."

Noah dropped the food onto the table and he took Chip's hands. His heart pounded in his chest as he looked past Chip to the crowd of his co-workers, who were all staring at him with the same, mushy smile.

"You've made me the happiest man on Earth," whispered Chip, staring deep into Noah's eyes.

"That's not possible because you've made me the happiest man on Earth."

Amy laughed and all of a sudden burst into tears. Chip also laughed, but nervously. He slowly lowered himself to one knee, forcing Noah's hand to clasp over his mouth.

"Noah," said Chip as he reached into the inside pocket of his suit jacket to pull out a small black box. "Will you marry me?"

Noah tried to speak, but a lump jammed in his throat as he held back the tears. Everybody was staring at him, waiting in anticipation for him to say something, anything. When he nodded frantically, wiping back the tears as a smile wider than he thought possible consumed his face, the crowd clapped and cheered.

"Of course I will," said Noah.

Chip slid the small silver band onto Noah's shaking finger, and it fit perfectly, as though it had been made for his finger, and his finger only.

"What was it you were saying about dreams coming true?" asked Chip.

Noah grabbed Chip and pulled him into a tight hug. He squinted through the tears at Amy, who was clapping her hands so fast and loud, she drowned out everybody else.

"You know people will already be placing bets on how long this marriage will last," whispered Noah.

"I know," said Chip. "I put ten quid on forever."

"I'm touched."

Noah's eyes wandered past Amy, to something new on the walls, and he spotted the '*art*' Amy had told him about. His heart sunk to the pit of his stomach, forcing him to cling on even tighter to Chip as the applause didn't show any signs of dying down.

"Please tell me why I'm looking at a canvas of what I think is my arse crack?" mumbled Noah through gritted teeth as he squinted at the photocopier picture.

"Merry Christmas."

ABOUT THE AUTHOR

Ashley John is a young gay author of gay romance novels. Living in the north of England with his fiancé and two cats, Ashley John spends his days writing down the voices he hears in his head. His books are primarily romance dramas with sprinklings of erotica and he has a knack for making you feel like you're living right beside the characters he creates. Ashley John is also a keen artist and he puts his artistic side to designing all of his own covers.

19649163R00092

Printed in Great Britain
by Amazon